Stranger on the Shore

Leon Franklin – Stranger on the Shore © 2021

Leon Franklin
Stranger on the Shore

A story of love, intimacy, deceit and intrigue.
Set in the sixties.

Leon Franklin – Stranger on the Shore © 2021

All rights reserved. No part of this book may be reproduced in any form without written permission of the Author.

ISBN: 9798514470303

To contact the author visit
www.leonfranklin.org

DEDICATION AND THANK YOU LIST

DEDICATION

This book is dedicated to all you wannabe writers out there who would love to write a book and for one reason or another have not achieved it. Whatever the reason my advice is - ***"Go for it!"*** If I can do it you can.

So go for it, that is, as long as you enjoy writing. If you feel unhappy, uncomfortable or find it a chore, leave it alone. The chances are it won't get published and if you haven't enjoyed doing it you will have gained nothing. That is just statistics and not me being pessimistic. Very few stories, especially by first-time writers, are ever published. Self-publishing is a different matter.

If my book does not get published, at least I have had the enjoyment of writing it. As I start to write this page it is 8th March 2013 and the main plot has been written. To all intents and purposes, my story is complete. I have of course read it and edited it many times already and although my story is fiction I have done many hours of research to get the events, dates and places as factual as possible. I will now keep my fingers crossed that with another two to three months' work including more editing following more research and proofreading it will be ready to meet the eagle eye of the literary agent and then the publisher. I have already achieved my aim of writing it. Now it's time for the difficult part. If you are reading this story and it is covered in a nice glossy paperback or strong hardback you will know I have achieved my next goal which is to get it published, or I have decided to self-publish.

It is now 2021. There have been many reasons why it has taken till now to actually publish. I was only turned down by one publisher but have now decided to self-publish through Amazon.

THANK YOU LIST

- Anyone who in any way has helped me to write this book
- All those people who helped me with my research*
- Family members who encouraged me, read the book and gave me feedback.
- My dear friend, Dorothy Smith, who sadly died in 2017. She read and gave encouraging feedback.
- James D Robinson another good friend has written and self-published many books. Some to be found on Amazon. I am grateful for his help with the publishing of this one.

*See Acknowledgements and Extras

APOLOGIES

Just want to say sorry to anyone who I have inadvertently missed out of the 'Thank You' or 'Acknowledgement' lists. If you have not had a mention and you feel you deserve one, please don't be shy, let me know and I will add you to the next reprint of my book.

NOTE

Some of the words written on these pages before Chapter 2 and after the epilogue were written at different times between 2011 and 2021. They show some of the build-up, thoughts, and things that were happening over those years up to the present day. I felt they should be left as they are.

MY NEXT BOOK

I have now started my next book called 'Runaway'. It should be ready for publication by February/March 2022 on Amazon.

CONTENTS

DEDICATIONS: Also a 'Thank You' list............................ 5

CONTENTS: Leon Franklin's Stranger on the Shore................. 7

PROLOGUE: An Introduction to Stranger on the Shore............. 9

CHAPTER ONE: Life and Death.. 15

CHAPTER TWO: Close Encounters of the Strange Kind............ 39

CHAPTER THREE: Precious Moments................................ 55

CHAPTER FOUR: Fond Memories..................................... 71

CHAPTER FIVE: Just Good Friends................................... 83

CHAPTER SIX: Close Encounter of the Intimate Kind.............. 91

CHAPTER SEVEN: The Truth Hurts.................................. 103

CHAPTER EIGHT: What Now?.. 119

CHAPTER NINE: Crosby's Christmas Party......................... 133

CHAPTER TEN: An Encounter of the Altogether Different Kind 147

CHAPTER ELEVEN: The Acceptance................................. 159

EPILOGUE: The Last Chapter... 173

REFERENCES: Relating to numbers within the text................ 189

THE AUTHOR: Leon Franklin... 191

ACKNOWLEDGEMENTS: and extras................................ 195

Leon Franklin – Stranger on the Shore © 2021

STRANGER ON THE SHORE

PROLOGUE:

An Introduction to Stranger on the Shore, by the author.

To use a similar phrase to the one Ernie Wise often used: 'This is a book what I wrote.'

Thank you for starting to read it and as Hughie Green used to say *"...and I mean that most sincerely folks."* Only I **really** do mean it sincerely. I hope you find it intriguing enough to read right to the end. I have read it many times but then I wrote it so I had to make sure it was correct. As I am getting on in years I also had to read it several times in order to remember what it was I had written?!?

Joking apart...
If you like surprises you should enjoy this story. It has some unexpected twists and turns along with drama, death, humour, loving sex, love lost and love found. It has deceit, hidden secrets, as well as spiritual, mysterious and romantic episodes. If that isn't quite enough for you, to add to all that, it has an interesting, entertaining and I think gripping storyline. If you agree or disagree, after reading it, then let me know via my website.

Any similarity to people, either living or dead, their stories, occupations, companies or businesses, is completely intentional. ONLY KIDDING!

No - whilst 'Stranger on the Shore' is fiction, the settings, places and times are factually accurate as far as it is humanly possible to make them. Fictional stories become much more believable, realistic and I think interesting when set in genuine places at known dates in history. However, it has not been my intention to use my life, or the lives of others (dead or alive), to base this story on. On the other hand, my life has been my only training in the art of writing. The 'University of Life' you may say. My life and my experiences including people I have met, books I have read and films I have seen are the only palettes of colour that I have to choose from when painting a picture.

If you want to read a little bit more about me, (and who wouldn't?) ☺ you can turn to the back now or leave it until you arrive at that point. Yes, your right! Leave it until you arrive at that point.

This story is set in the North East of England and reading this book will immerse you mainly in the 1960s with some mention of the fifties as well. If you lived through the 60's it will bring back many fond memories. If you are too young to remember the 60's, that's fine, I am sure you will still find it very interesting and entertaining. You will also feel quite at home because those times were so important they will never be forgotten. Parents, teachers and television will have given you a great deal of knowledge about those days. The music, art, fashion and all things cultural made and still make a huge impression on the direction of the people, and of the country, that is Great Britain.

Why 'Stranger' on the Shore? Well, I really do not fully know the answer to that. I have often wanted to write a story. I feel so privileged to have lived through the 60s my story was almost certain to be set in that time period. Then about two years ago one day out of the blue, no pun intended, I got the inspiration for a story based on this chap meeting a stranger at the seaside. Then into my head came that haunting and most beautiful melody by Acker Bilk entitled 'Stranger on the Shore'. When I started the book I had no idea it was going to take me this long to write. I have only just recently knuckled down to it. I have taken it from one and a half chapters written in I think 2011 to its completion within about the first six months of 2013. Publishing date 2021.

I know that authors are often asked 'how did you come up with the names of the characters?' So here is my answer. On most occasions, I simply used the first name that came into my head but the other thing I did was to use normal, everyday, names that you would have certainly heard in the '60s and to this day for that matter. I avoided names like Tarquin, Gerard and Alicia. Don't get me wrong I am not having a go at anyone with those names they were just not right for my book.

This book, I now believe, will be just the first in a series of books all with different stories set in the 1960s and inspired by a 'Top of the Pops' type record. I want to make it plain that I did not first choose Acker Bilks record and then start writing the story. It was the other way around but for the next and successive books that is exactly what I intend to do. For each book in the rest of this series, I will first choose a well-known hit of the '60s and then, if it inspires me, formulate and build a story around it. As yet, as I continue to write this prologue in April 2013, I have no clue as to what that will be. I need to concentrate on completely finishing this one first. Suggestions welcome via my website email address.

We, therefore, have a tune whose title is associated with the story so I hope that with permission if permission is needed, it will be used as a theme tune if ever a film or play is made of it. Meanwhile, you may, while you are reading, wish to have Acker's masterpiece playing in the background on an i-pod, i-phone or i-player. Perhaps even on an i-ron. I am sure in this age of technology that will be possible. After all, you can now have music coming out of your sofa. If you have no means of listening to the tune 'Stranger on the Shore' you may like to whistle or hum it, at least, when you start each new chapter. If, and I doubt it, you have no idea what the tune sounds like, go to 'extras' towards the back of the book or to my website for a link which will enable you to listen online.

To some readers horror (when I carried out a pre-publication survey) there are times when I will, as the author, speak directly to you to add something to the story. It may be just a joke or a comment about the situation or events in the 1960s. So that you are not confused between the storyline and my utterances I will use this kind of typeface and put square brackets [like this] around it. This is just the way I write and is a similar style to the actor or actress that looks straight into the camera and talks to the viewing audience as in Miranda and Mrs Brown's Boys and some stage plays. References[1] like the number one I have just used will allow you to find out more information towards the back of the book.

A few comments below relate to television. If you wish to read more of my ramblings I have a blog on my website called 'Too Close for Comfort' which you may like to read.

I am a realist so I know that there is a good possibility that my book may only find its way to a publisher's waste bin. However, I am also a positive person and you need to have good positive thoughts and think big for good things to happen. Therefore if it is a success and someone decides to make a film or television play out of it, I must insist that when the story takes us back or forward in time the viewer is kept properly informed. I am quite annoyed when I am watching a play on television and I haven't a clue where we are or what time zone we are in. Are we before or after the event or in the present? We sometimes do not know for sure if the character had been thinking, dreaming or was in the present. During this story, I will keep you informed of when and where I have taken you by using this font and placing the dates and places inside square brackets. For example as I write this part, today's information about me would read [Leon Franklin's Studio, Thursday 3rd October 2013] I do want anyone watching the television play to be just as clear about the time zones as I have made them, for you the reader, among the pages and paragraphs of my very own first book....

'Stranger on the Shore.'
Enjoy...

CHAPTER ONE: Life and Death.

[Scarborough Beach, early morning, 10th July 1963]

"*HUH-HOOO, HUH-HOOO*" came the sound of heavy breathing as Neil struggled to catch his breath and at the same time keep up the pace of his regular morning run. 'Time to pause for a breather' Neil thought as he approached his usual resting place. It was a wall that separated Scarborough beach from Foreshore Road, not far from the Life Boat Station[1] and the harbour. He usually started and finished his run from there. Providing the tide was out he would set off along the sands heading away from the Life Boat Station.

Getting back to his flat in Eastborough, on his return journey, was a fairly steep climb so he certainly needed a rest at this point before starting up the hill. He sucked in the fresh sea air and it felt good. The exercise was very important to him, more so than for most. Neil was recovering from a head-on car crash in which his wife Fiona had died. It happened on the 9th August 1961 and whilst he remembers very little of that day, it is a date he will never forget.

He was doing very well now physically, having recovered from broken bones and severe wounds to both legs. Even worse were head and chest injuries that left him in a coma and on life support for the best part of three months.

Neil, born in Middlesbrough in 1937, grew up in the Northeast of England and had little conscious memory of World War Two. It had though, left an impression on him as both his parents were killed, his father in the services in 1941 and his mother by a bomb in 1942. Neil and his older sister Jennifer, usually called Jenny, were moved to Northallerton and brought up by their Aunty Annie. She also sadly died, in her sleep, in 1956 after a long and worthwhile life culminating in the nurture of Neil and Jenny, her nephew and niece. Gladly by that time, they were adults and she had lived long enough to see the wonderful results of her love and guardianship.

It was good fortune that Aunty Annie lived in Northallerton as it proved to be a safer place, away from the main targets of enemy bombers. There were many factories and other targets for German bombers in and around Middlesbrough. In Northallerton, some say, you were more likely to be killed by one of our own aeroplanes as they limped back from the action to one of the nearby airfields. Many of them were so shot up they crashed before they managed to land safely, some only just making it onto the airstrip.

Despite the war and the effects of losing both parents, Jenny and Neil enjoyed their childhood. This was mainly thanks to Aunty Annie, who loved them dearly. Realising what a traumatic blow they had had to their childhood, she went out of her way to try and make it up to them. She did not spoil them, in fact, she was quite strict but had the right balance of love and discipline to nurture what became two very decent adults and good citizens. Neil and Jenny naturally grew very close to each other emotionally, yet both became very independent and able to look after themselves and each other. Their experiences also left them with a fairly traditional outlook on life.

Their Aunty Annie was a staunch churchgoer attending All Saints Parish Church in the High Street. Naturally, Neil and Jenny went with her, at first as part of the Sunday school and this Christian teaching helped to give them some very useful lessons about relationships and life in general. It also gave them faith to help them through some of the bad times when food and money were short. Neil's belief in Jesus as his friend had grown strong, helped him through and would continue to do so in the difficult times ahead.

Neil was now a slim, though not skinny, 5' 7", clean shaven and quite good looking, young man. Always smartly dressed, he had dark brown eyes and hair to match. He often altered his hair to reflect the current fashion, sometimes short back and sides, then a DA[2]. Sometimes he wore it 'Elvis-like' and for a while had a Beatle cut.

Before the accident Neil had been quite fit, often playing football, cricket or taking regular cycling trips. Since the accident, he had worked hard to get back to his usual level of fitness. He was almost back to his active self and his mental and emotional state was improving but he still had many moments of sad reflection.

Neil and Fiona had been very much in love since way back when. They were school children when they first met. Neil was now twenty-six years of age and Fiona would have been twenty-four. Tragedy had struck on the A167, between Darlington and Northallerton, when an out of control Jaguar hurtled towards their Morris Minor, causing the head-on crash, or so Neil had been told. He had read a few newspaper cuttings but most of the story had been printed while he was in a hospital bed, almost at the point of death. Once he was well enough, he could not acquire any substantive news reports and had to rely on what others told him. [In those days, there was no internet, not even a mobile phone. In fact, even household phones were comparatively rare due to the expense.] Those he managed to persuade to tell him about the crash were, for obvious reasons, a little reluctant to go into detail.

[The Hospital Mid-November 1961]

Ten weeks after the accident and it was still 'touch and go' for Neil as to the long term prognosis. The doctors were quite pleased with most of the physical signs of healing. He was making progress on his long road to recovery. Although he was no longer on life support he was still in a coma.

"Is he going to pull through?" asked Jenny, standing in the corridor near to Neil's room, having managed to catch up with the doctor in charge of his case. She was the only relative able to visit the hospital on a regular basis. Actually, she was one of the few relatives Neil had left.

"It is very difficult in situations like this. He is breathing on his own now," answered the doctor, adding, *"So the signs are good. Apart from his brain function all the other parts of his body appear to be repairing and should, in time, work normally, although he will need lots of support and physiotherapy."* He

thought for a moment and continued. *"That is if he,* **err when** *he regains consciousness."*

There was a long silence. They looked at each other. The doctor wishing he had been more articulate and Jenny with a look on her face of enquiring horror.

Jenny thought, 'had it been a slip of the tongue or did he really mean *'if'* he regains consciousness?' The doctor could see Jenny was getting upset and the silence was broken by both starting to speak at the same time…

"Look …," the doctor began but hesitated not wanting to talk over Jenny.

"Tell me?" Jenny was about to pose a question but allowed the doctor to continue.

"The brain is a complicated organ," he said, having been given the opportunity to speak, *"until Neil starts to respond we will not fully know the extent of any damage. Remember to talk to him when you visit. A patient's hearing and subconscious can still be working even though they cannot respond. Give him hope for his future and reasons to get better."*

Thankfully, in some ways, Neil was left with a scant recollection of the accident and at this stage, was completely unaware of Fiona's death.

Neil's awakening was not sudden; he couldn't speak and showed very little movement. Jenny was called to the hospital when the staff first noticed signs that he was starting to come around. The flickering of an eyelid, the twitch of a finger, were all small, but good signs. She stayed with him for hours, during which time he was still only just-to-say conscious or in deep sleep.

"You're going to be fine," encouraged Jenny holding Neil's hand. Leaning closer she added, *"You're getting stronger every day."* She then leant closer still and kissed him just above his eyebrow on the little bit of skin showing below the bandage that still adorned his head. Sitting back

down she continued to talk to him. *"Bill and the kids send their love. They are looking forward to playing cricket with you once again."* Bill Jackson was Jenny's husband. Being older than Neil it was just natural that she got married before he did.

Jenny remembered her first visit to the hospital and being shocked at seeing Neil so badly injured. Once she had finally recovered, calmed down and regained control of her emotions, she stood looking at his motionless figure. As she stood looking him up and down she thought 'there is so much of his body covered in bandage that he resembles an Egyptian Mummy.' Jenny was so happy that she could gradually see fewer bandages being used as the time went by and now, real signs of getting a response. One of the things that concerned her was, the longer the periods of consciousness, the more frustration showed on Neil's face.

Several hours after showing his first signs of coming around he began to move his mouth. Words were not forthcoming, in fact, to start with there was no sound, just mouth movements. Then gradually incoherent noises, groans and sighs turned into obvious efforts to make words.

"Why does his face seem to distort? Is he in pain?" enquired Jenny of the attending nurse.

"We think it's just the frustration of not being able to communicate," replied the nurse as she changed Neil's drip which was feeding him intravenously. *"He is probably trying, in his mind, but not yet well enough to actually speak."*

A little later Jenny, still at his bedside, read her Woman's Own magazine and paused from time to time to read him a joke or an interesting passage. Her attention was soon drawn to Neil's efforts to speak.
After a long pause, with very little movement, Neil appeared to muster what little strength he had to blurt out, **"F... Fia... Fiona?"** Jenny dropped her magazine.

That first word was only the one word, but a word with such meaning. Embedded in it were the unspoken questions: 'Is she OK? Where is she?' He had insufficient strength to say more than that one word, never mind to ask questions, but he had still managed to communicate his 'must-have' piece of information. At that moment in time, it was the only thing he was interested in or cared about. It had taken such an effort on his part that he again slumped back into what appeared to be a semi-consciousness or deep sleep.

There was silence. Jenny felt delighted, relieved and guilty all at the same time. Delighted at his first spoken word, relieved that she did not have to answer and then guilty for feeling that relief. Of course, she had hoped and prayed for him to wake up. 'Not knowing how to answer is understandable' she convinced herself, 'just how I am going to tell him Fiona is dead, I do not know?' Of course, she realised that there would come a time when she could no longer put off the inevitable.

Jenny felt a great loss at Fiona's death; she was like a sister, a dear sister and close friend. There were many tearful and testing moments in the Jackson household since the accident. She arranged the funeral on Neil's behalf after consulting with Fiona's parents and could only hope it would meet with his approval. Naturally, the funeral took place in All Saints Parish Church and Fiona was buried in the local cemetery which is near to the church on the High Street. It was a very sad occasion. Funerals usually are sad but to add to the heartache of Fiona's death, for those in attendance, their thoughts were also with her missing husband lying in a hospital bed fighting for his life.

'If I am so affected by this tragedy, I cannot begin to imagine what Neil will go through when he hears the news' she thought as she sat beside his bed. 'Still weak and tired recovering from the trauma, confused at losing ten weeks from his life, then being hit like a battering ram with the news of his wife's death.' She shuddered to think about how he would react and how it would affect his recovery.

Neil and Fiona's relationship was very special. Not just a married couple but they had also been childhood sweethearts, best friends and lovers. Jenny tried but found it difficult in her mind's eye to visualise the pain and mental anguish Neil was about to be put through. 'This will rip him apart' she thought.

Not all marriages are as perfect but Neil and Fiona had truly become one. Their love, respect and devotion were very strong. Their relationship was not just one of lust, although there had been plenty of that, but true deep satisfying love that is so rare. Theirs was an eternal love, which would remain long after the last remnants of lust disappeared. An eternal love, as the description implies, that will last even after death.

A few hours later Jenny could see that it was time to break the tragic news, to a still very ill patient. She could see by the obvious anguish on his face that not telling him was just not morally correct. Plucking up more courage than she had ever needed before, and thinking it best to say it quickly, Jenny said, fighting back the tears. *"I am so sorry Neil. Fiona has died."* She continued in a vain attempt to blunt his pain by adding, *"She didn't suffer....the doctors assured me... it was so fast she did not feel any pain."* Now both were crying out loud. She wanted to run away thinking that her emotional state was making things worse for him. But she couldn't leave him in his hour of need; overcoming her urge to dash away she comforted him until they were both cried out.

Jenny stayed longer and visited more often and gradually coaxed and helped him to improve his movement and speech. Neil's emotions were running wild and he reacted in many different ways each day. He was sometimes a good patient and then the worst patient ever. He was very polite one minute to everyone around him and then would suddenly treat the nurses with contempt. His other visitors included the Vicar of All Saints and his good friend Dave, best man at his wedding. On one occasion he greeted them with joy, yet on the next visit, he virtually ignored them and became very aloof.

His emotional state ranged from wishing he had died in the accident to wanting to get better and strangle the driver of the other car. The main thing that affected his thinking finally rested on knowing the love Fiona has for him. Such a love, that can never die, would only want him to get better, stronger and live a full life. No way would she have wanted him to grow bitter, wither and die, commit suicide or spend his life being miserable.

[A little more background information]

After being discharged from the hospital Neil spent some time at Jenny's house to recuperate. The children, Kenneth and Elizabeth, had him playing games again within a few weeks. Whilst at first he got tired easily and he did need plenty of rest, the exercise both to his body and mind was beneficial. Love and attention were what he needed and Jenny and her family ensured he got bucket loads of that.

Once he was well enough to go back home, it was such a very different feeling walking through the door to an empty house. Still full of furniture and household goods but empty because it was Fiona-less. Crying was something Neil did often, but less and less as time went by. Not because he loved Fiona any less, certainly not, it's just that as with most humans, as time goes by his emotions naturally became calmer and easier to control.

[This is probably where the saying 'time heals' gets its origin. Deep mental wounds, caused by such a loss like Neil's, never heal completely and can at any time, and often did, burst wide open to reveal a bleeding broken heart.]

After their marriage, Neil and Fiona found a house that they loved in Quaker Lane, Northallerton. As it happened they had lived not far from there as children and went to the same school. Their house was nothing fancy but to them, it was the place, perhaps the palace, they loved to come home to. This was only because they knew that, at the end of each working day, they were coming home to each other.

Knowing that he was hurting, and that was the last thing Fiona would want for him, he decided to move house. He chose a ground floor flat situated in Eastborough, within walking distance from the seashore, in Scarborough. Together they had often visited Scarborough and other places along the Northeast coast. They had many adventures and shared plenty of precious moments in that area. Sometimes they visited one of the many caravan parks and sometimes rented a holiday flat, or stayed at a bed and breakfast establishment.

Having already lost people who were close to him, Neil was aware that everyone deals with grief in a different way. 'One should never judge another's actions just because they do not seem to conform,' he reassured himself. 'Others may think they would react differently in the same situation, but moving was the right thing for me.' Yes, he had moved to one of their favourite seaside haunts which would be a constant reminder of her. The reason for moving was not because the house in Northallerton reminded him of Fiona. On the contrary, he continued to fill many hours thinking about the good times they had shared.

There were three main reasons for moving. Firstly, because every time he stepped in through their front door, in Quaker Lane, he half expected to experience the usual warm, loving greeting he once received. Deep inside Neil knew, 'I will never feel that warm welcome again.' So he tried hard to resign himself to the situation. Yet on the surface, on every homecoming, he still kept wishing, praying, hoping, expecting, all to no avail. This was so hard for him to bear. Secondly, they had planned to start a family so chose the house especially because it had extra rooms. Finally, the house was too expensive for him living on his own.

For a long time, he had some very sad and lonely moments. He would suddenly catch a glimpse of someone in a crowd who looked like Fiona, his heart jumped with glee and he would have to stop himself from calling out her name. He would head towards the sighting to get a closer look but would soon realise the silliness of what he was doing. For that one or two fleeting seconds, he had hope, the hope that they were about to be reunited, only to have his hopes dashed immediately and confounded by the absurdity of his thinking and actions. That is until the next time it happened.

At night his dreams were bittersweet. He would often dream they were in each other's arms only to wake up to reality. He would often dream he was looking for her as if she was just in a different town or house. He would ask her why she was living somewhere else and never seemed to get an answer.

His dreams were so real he could smell her perfume and hear her voice. He could see her beautiful body and feel her soft skin in his arms. Even though the pain of waking up to reality was hard to bear he often tried desperately to get back to sleep to be with her again for a few more precious moments.

One thing is for sure, his life without Fiona would never be the same. Neil would never be the same.

[It has been said that when someone, very close to you dies, and you have shared a love passionately and deeply, you will never be the same again. The reason is that the one who dies takes with them the parts of your character they loved the most.]

[Back with Neil still 10th July 1963]

He continued his long, and now slow, trek back to the flat walking up the steeply sloping road. He was happy with the way his run had gone and felt pleased with his improvement but always allowed himself to walk the last but most strenuous part of the journey. It was, perhaps, symbolic of the strenuous journey he would tread during the next part of his life.

[Newcastle, 1954]

A hundred miles away, at a different time, in another part of the North East, were two people completely unrelated to the character previously introduced, yet with one thing in common, they were all recovering from emotional and physical pain through the death of a loved one.

Jeffrey Robinson was a very successful architect working in the City of Newcastle. Mary, his wife, was also well educated and quite well off financially coming from a family of business people. She appeared to be in good health but just like many of her friends she was a smoker and a heavy one at that. I do not mean heavy as in fat but heavy as in smoking a lot of cigarettes. She was not a chain smoker but was not far off. They never wanted for anything, in the early years, living in a beautifully situated house in the best part of Newcastle with a strong and loving relationship.

I said earlier that they never wanted for anything. That was not quite true, for after having tried for many months to produce a child, their lives were devastated, just over a year ago, when Mary miscarried in the ninth week of pregnancy. They both so yearned for children it physically and mentally hurt when it seemed they were going to be robbed of this gift. Those were dark days and although Jeff in no way blamed Mary, splits started to appear. No one was to blame but the strong bond between them had started to erode.

Now, a year later, much to their delight, Mary was pregnant. Jeff and Mary were now very happy after a long and worrying period of gestation.

They got through those dark days. Whilst Jeff was a good husband, Mary was the one to steady the ship when things got rough. She was such a good wife. She loved her life in Newcastle and adored her husband. She was very dutiful and always went that extra mile to take care of Jeff, manage the domestic arrangements and keep their large house immaculately clean without a maid or home help that her neighbours boasted about.

She was genuinely a good person, always willing to help a neighbour. For example; sensing the eighty-year-old lady, who lived across the road, found it difficult to get to the shops Mary purposely befriended her. Her name was Josie but due to the age difference and out of respect she started to call her Aunty Josie though of course, they were no relation. Mary would often call in to see her or telephone to check she was OK. Josie was so grateful knowing that Mary was only a phone call away. Mary was quite happy to go out of her way to take Josie shopping in the car or even go shopping for her if, age-related, aches and pains made her feel unwell.

Whilst the last few months had been a worrying time, due to her previous miscarriage, the fact that she was now almost at the point of reaching full term, allowed their confidence to grow. So the divisions that had started to appear in their marriage were gradually healing as Mary's time drew near. You could measure Jeff's happiness at the thoughts of becoming a father by the broadness of his smile which he now carried around with him every day.

The due date had come and gone; the birth was expected a week ago. Bags were packed, plans were in place, the nursery had been made ready, clothes had been purchased and gifts had been received, all in neutral colours. Jeff even bought a large box of cigars ready to hand out to his colleagues at work. It was all systems go and the waiting seemed like a lifetime to the expectant couple. Jeff and Mary had waited such a long time already and had gone through the pain of losing, what would have been, their first child. They were outwardly and naturally very happy but because of their past experience, they had also gone through most of the nine months with a sort of heavy feeling in the pit of their stomachs. Deep inside there were doubts and concerns gnawing, nagging and eating away at their very being. The longer the pregnancy continued without any problems the more these doubts faded but now the waiting was difficult to bear. Joy, excitement and expectation was now fighting for a place in their hearts.

"I think, she or he is going to be a lazy baby," Mary commented light heartedly as she stubbed out her last cigarette for the day.

"Why is that honey?" replied Jeff as they climbed into bed.

"Well!" she said, *"To start with – it's late and it hasn't done much kicking today."*

"He may be tired dear. He will be fine," said Jeff, in a reassuring manner. He planted a kiss on her cheek, gently patted her bump and reiterated, *"He's probably just tired; I know I am! Goodnight honey."* Turned over and went to sleep.

Jeff, as you can probably tell was hoping for a boy. Whilst that would have been his choice if he had one, believe me, it did not really matter, all he wanted was to make their marriage complete and become a father.

It was a restless night for Mary. Jeff was sleeping like a log as usual. Last time they held a dinner party Mary told her guests, *"He sleeps like a log."* Then joked, *"I am surprised he doesn't wake up in the fireplace."*

About three o'clock in the morning it was action stations.

"Jeff, Jeff, wake up, wake up it's started!" Mary screamed as she held her abdomen with one hand and at the same time shook Jeff with the other. Jeff woke up and jumped out of bed quicker than he had ever done before.

"Eh, err, OK! OK!" said Jeff, as he came to his senses and started towards the door. *"I'll telephone for an ambulance."*

Mary was groaning with the pain.

Jeff stopped momentarily, *"How often are the contractions?"* asked Jeff, thinking 'they are bound to ask me on the phone.'

"I don't know I have just woken up and can feel the pain." Then with a sudden sickening realisation, Mary shouted, almost screamed, **"Jeff!**

There are no contractions I can just feel this horrendous pain."

Jeff ran down the stairs to the sound of Mary groaning, picked up the phone and quickly dialled 999.

"Please help - come quickly, my wife is in labour and I think there is something wrong." Tears started to fill Jeff's eyes as he realised that contraction pains can be quite painful but that there should be periods in between when nothing is happening and the level of pain, he could hear Mary suffering, could not be normal.

Mary still crying in pain, shouted, **"Hurry, hurry Jeff, tell them to hurry."** She had not been able to move from her bed, the pain was so severe. Jeff had been up and down the stairs several times feeling helpless, not knowing what to do and was now, after what seemed like an age, opening the front door to let in the ambulance men.

"I think my waters have broken!" Mary exclaimed, still crying in pain, as the ambulance men entered the bedroom. There was a look of shock and horror on all their faces, even the ambulance men who were used to dealing with some nasty incidents recoiled. Their reaction reflected the horror that was revealed when the blankets were pulled back. Blood was covering the sheets and had soaked Mary's night clothes, they knew straightaway the danger she was in.

At that point, they really needed to go and get a stretcher from the ambulance but realising how dangerous the signs were for Mary's health, as well as the baby's, to save time the larger and stronger of the two ambulance men grabbed Mary in his arms and rushed her downstairs. *"Let's go Joe!"* and with that all of them sped off down the street in the ambulance, full pelt, with bells ringing, to get to the hospital as soon as possible.

Although it was the last thing on his mind, Jeff had locked the front door, but only because the lock works automatically without a key until you want to get back in. It wasn't until later that Jeff realised he had no key with him, in fact, he had his trousers on over his pyjamas. He would have to break in, but as his mind was on that of his wife and son's desperate and dangerous condition, he spent no more than a fleeting second on any other problem that came to mind.

Mary had to have a caesarean operation and their much-anticipated child; their much loved and longed for child - was stillborn. It was a girl, they had not chosen a name and now they were so distraught it never entered their heads to name her. They finally settled on Molly in time for the funeral. It is said that the name 'Molly' has two meanings 'bitterness' and 'longed-for child.' The first part of the meaning reflected their angst at having lost her and the second part is obvious.

Everyone found it difficult to understand what could have caused this devastating death, of their unborn baby in the womb. Mary was also close to death having required several pints of blood before they were even able to start the operation. If it had not been for the swift action of the ambulance men, Jeff could have lost both of them.

The doctors explained to Jeff and Mary that their daughter's death was due to 'Placenta Previa'. In layman's language that means the placenta had burst open because it was positioned below the baby's head preventing a natural birth. This meant that Molly had been starved of oxygen and Mary had almost bled to death. The doctors aware of her smoking habit did explain that it was highly likely the cause of Molly's death and said that they could see no medical reason why Mary should not be able to have children in the future but that she must really be determined to stop smoking. *"Yet… on the other hand, do they want to put themselves through the possibility of all that stress and heartache again?"*

The answer from both of them was a very, very reluctant but perfectly understandable, *"No."*

Multiply the heartache they had already gone through losing their first child through miscarriage by a thousand and you will not come close to what life was like for Mary and Jeff in the days following their recent loss.

At first, they were supportive of each other but gradually the same rifts and splits that surfaced before, once again, marred their normally good life. Quite how their marriage survived is nothing short of a miracle. Jeff nearly lost his job because his heart and soul were no longer in his work. He could no longer get excited about anything. Mary also was very morose and did not have the same get up and go. Looking after the house and home seemed for a long time to become an unwanted and unnecessary chore. There were no more dinner parties, after all, what was there to celebrate?

To add to her woes, Aunty Josie died of a heart attack two months after Mary came out of the hospital. A very sad lady had lost her second child, a neighbour who had become a friend and was now in great danger of losing her husband all within a very short time. Add to that the torment of giving up smoking for her health sake really depressed her.

Jeff was summoned to appear before the head of architecture and given a real roasting for shoddy work and bad timekeeping. It was his good work in the past and excellent employment history that saved him getting the chop. This jolted him into action and he was determined not to let his emotional feelings affect his work from that day forward. It was tough though because sometimes, especially now his marriage was failing, he didn't even feel *life* was worth continuing, never mind his job.

Mary and Jeff being of the old school stayed together despite their problems.

[In those days people did stay together through tough times. Nowadays it seems you only have to go BOO! To get them

separating. In fact, nowadays, on many occasions, they do not even bother to go through the married bit.]

However, their life and relationship were never the same. Arguments occurred over things that would normally have been no problem. Things that would have been talked through amiably and lovingly in times gone by were now like friction points that set them at each other's throats, figuratively speaking, because they were never physically violent towards each other.

Mary, despite the problems, was usually a very positive person and slowly but surely regained some of her inner strength. She tried on many occasions to help Jeff to become his old self and heal their wounds but without much success. Sex was a thing of the past and even kisses were few and far between and not much more enjoyable than kissing a dead fish when they did happen. Despite Mary's heroic efforts, they struggled on in what was really now just an existence.

[September 1955]

Whilst money was no problem, all their other problems meant they hadn't had a holiday for a long time. Neither were they in any mood for a holiday, well, at least not with each other. However, a friend, Gareth Jones, had offered them the use of his holiday cottage on Barry Island, South Wales, at the end of the month. It was near the end of the season and just happened to be available then. It used to be his own house but he rented it out since moving to the North East of England. Reluctantly, in some ways, they agreed to it. Despite their misgivings about the amount of enjoyment they would have due to their broken relationship, they decide pragmatically that they would go, as both were in desperate need of a break. So they took advantage of Gareth's kind offer.

Oddly, from that very moment, the atmosphere seemed, just so very slightly, to become lighter. Perhaps it was the first time, for a very long time, they now had something to look forward to. They later actually started to enjoy, without argument, discussing their holiday plans together.

"What a lovely little cottage," remarked Mary on arrival.

"It certainly is," replied Jeff, *"and just look at that view from the window."*

The weather was good considering it was late in the season and the raging storms between Mary and Jeff were now mainly on the distant horizon with just the odd thundery shower spoiling their relationship from time to time.

"Gareth told me that there are some lovely beaches in Barry and the surrounding area," Jeff explained to Mary. *"**And...** he said there were spectacular limestone cliffs on the Glamorgan Coast with pebbly but **secluded** beaches."*

Mary, still looking out of the window, mused, 'hum - that sounds as if Jeff intends to make this a holiday to remember.' She had detected a touch of mischief in his voice and his emphasis on the word 'secluded.' However, they did not venture onto the beach mainly because of what Jeff said next.

His voice changed and became very stern *"We must be very careful to check the tides before we take to the beach."*

"Why?" inquired Mary turning towards him. She realised that you had to be careful of the tide on most beaches but wondered, 'Why seemingly so important here?'

"There is a difference of 50 feet between high and low tide," stressed Jeff.

"Wow! That is scary," she agreed and could now understand.

"Whilst on the map this area can look like the outlet of the river Severn it is, in fact, the Bristol Channel, in other words, the sea!" Jeff pointed out. *"Gareth reckons it is the second largest rise in tide in the world."*

They did everything most people do on holiday and were much more relaxed than they had been at home. To a great extent, it was as if they had left all their problems back in Newcastle. They walked and talked, went to the fair and the amusements. They went site seeing and really enjoyed their time together.

One evening they decided to go to the local pub. They just fancied a drink and possibly a bar meal. They liked a drink but were not regulars. It turned out to be a wonderful evening, there were some local entertainers, food available and it was very busy. The atmosphere was just wonderful and despite the hustle and bustle, they were also able to talk when they sat close. They made jokes and found themselves laughing together, not only enjoying the venue and the ambience but more importantly, each other.

As they walked back to the cottage arm in arm, that night, felt like no other. It was a clear, cloudless and very romantic starlit night. It could have been the unsaid agreement of a truce. It could have been the relaxation of being on holiday away from it all. It could also have something to do with the addition of alcohol. Whatever it was, all inhibitions and aggravations had gone. Once through the cottage door, the splendid evening was to be topped off with an even more splendid night, as Jeff led Mary by the hand upstairs. It was a long time since they last made love and they had almost forgotten how good it felt. This night reminded them just what they had been missing. The wow factor was back.

The build-up produced slight tremors, like the early signs of an impending volcanic eruption, to which loud cries of delight, gasps and groans could be heard. Their bodies began to writhe, heads became light and started to spin as the earth began to move with even greater intensity from kissing, touching and penetration. Their natural human pent up desire to make love, which had lain dormant for a very long time, was like a huge build-up of white-hot magma below the surface. This desire having been suppressed by their almost broken marriage was now free to explode completely out of control. Almost without warning, the eruption began and they were soon engulfed in a pyroclastic flow, of sexual pleasure, relief, delight and satisfaction.

Needless to say, they also enjoyed the rest of their holiday and came back very refreshed if not just a little tired. Their train crash of a marriage was not suddenly the Orient Express but was at least back on the tracks.

[Mid November 1955]

Whilst it would not be true to say things were now completely back to normal, spirits had definitely lifted since their holiday on Barry Island and especially since that very special evening when they got closer than they had been for a very long time. There were now some happier moments, there was more laughter, they even arranged a dinner party as a thank you to their friend for the loan of the holiday cottage.

Jeff got home from work one Thursday evening in January. Nothing unusual about that, except that he could not understand why all the lights were out. 'Perhaps she is still at the shops or with a friend.' He thought, as he switched on the hallway light and walked through into the lounge.

"Mary?" he said questioningly when he realised she was sitting in the lounge in the dark. *"What's up? Why are you sitting in the dark?"* She remained, just sitting still staring blankly into space. **"Mary!"** he spoke a little louder as he sat down in the chair almost opposite.

She slowly turned her face towards him, *"I have been to the doctors."*

"Why, what's the matter, why the doctors?" he said leaning forward towards her.

"I haven't been feeling too good these past few weeks. I didn't think it would be much so I did not say anything to you." A short pause then, *"I am glad you are sitting down Jeff."* Jeff's stomach turned and several horrible scenarios passed through his mind.

"Tell me, what is it?" The suspense was becoming unbearable. He sat back and tried to relax. They were just starting to get their lives back together. 'What cruel burden is life about to lay upon us now?' he wondered.

There was a long pause. Neither spoke. They just sat looking at each other through the near darkness. Mary seemed to take a few deep breaths before she answered.

"I am six weeks pregnant."

Another long silence, neither knew how to react within nor did they know how the other would react. They seemed very disturbed. A time like this that would normally herald outbursts of joy was instead greeted with silence. They did not dare to believe everything would be alright. They could only; it seems from their experience, look forward to more pain and heartache.

It was probably just a matter of seconds, but it seemed like hours before either made any move or broke the silence. Mary was first to break when her inner turmoil spilt out and she began to cry.

"What are we going to do Jeff?" Mary sobbed and pleaded. Jeff came to her side, went down on his knees to be on the same level, put his arm around her, laid his head on her shoulder and also began to cry. *"I don't know, I don't know, I **really** do not know."*

They stayed in each other's arms crying until the tears dried up. Despite the thoughts of what might be in store, Jeff was horrified when Mary told him a doctor had offered a termination as a solution. One of the doctors had whispered this suggestion into her ear and secreted a card with his name and number on into her hand.

[The law was a little hazy on the subject of abortion at this time and it was certainly illegal unless it could be clearly proved to be vital in order to save the life of the mother.]

After much soul searching, they decided that perhaps at last life, fate or God was giving them another chance to be really happy. They didn't appear to have any particular faith or beliefs. When they filled in a form they did what most other English people do. Where it asks your faith they put C of E yet like most, they were not practising Christians. They were just part of the hatch-'em, match-'em and despatch-'em brigade, only attending church on special occasions[3].

They reminisced about how their lives used to be, when they were courting and first married. How they always wanted to have children. Being told by the doctor that she was six weeks into the pregnancy they worked back and realised she must have conceived while on holiday on Barry Island. That means a rough due date for the birth would be June 1956. Eventually, after much discussion and a lot more kissing and cuddling than usual, they concluded that they just had to go with the flow. They would certainly not pre-empt events by using the option of termination for what might happen in the future, especially as this appeared to be against the law. They did, however, decide, in later discussions with the doctor, that Mary should be admitted to hospital early and go for an elective caesarean section about two weeks before the baby was due.

Deep down despite their fears and past experience they were both harbouring seeds of delight that this time they might actually achieve their aim of becoming parents. Several months later, following a fairly trouble free pregnancy, Mary gave birth to a healthy eight-pound three-ounce baby boy. Naturally, they called him Barry. All that time they did not dare to celebrate, at least until the moment, following the operation, when mother and baby were declared well.

Then everyone let their hair down at the Christening party. As you can imagine, Jeff was in especially good form. He explained to everyone, rather to Mary's embarrassment, why they called him Barry.

He then said, *"I am just glad we didn't holiday in the town of Llanfairpwllgwyngyllgogerychwyrndrobwyll-llantysiliogogogoch."*

They all laughed hysterically and were very impressed at his articulation.
Without telling anyone he had learned to say it (well nearly perfectly) from his friend Gareth, who was sworn to secrecy. Jeff practised it every day and did not tell Gareth why he wanted to learn it, so even he enjoyed the punch line.

Needless to say, the cigars were given out, champagne flowed and everything was wonderful in the Robinson family. Mary was an awesome, loving, mother and now devoted her life to her baby, husband and home. Home really felt like home as it had never done before.

Jeff was an excellent father and husband. He was on top of the world and regularly took every opportunity to play with Barry. As his son got older and developed, he introduced him to new experiences. First, the swings in the park, then toy building bricks, followed on his third birthday by the purchase of Hornby 00 gauge model railway.

"He is only three years old," protested Mary laughingly.

"He will grow into it," answered Jeff, realising he had been rumbled. He had always wanted a train set as a child. *"Look he loves it,"* he said, pointing to the way Barry was engrossed in what was happening. Unfortunately, Barry's hand-eye coordination wasn't quite practised enough for the task he was trying to perform. He sat near the table, in his special chair, eating his dinner yet constantly missed his mouth. His eyes and head followed the train around the track while his hand spooned food from his bowl. It hit many places, but not his mouth, rolling down his bib, legs and seat before dropping to the floor.

Over the next year or two, Barry grew up a happy and very healthy infant. He was smart, good looking with a cheeky grin. Despite being a little mischievous, he was so lovable with it.

There was now no turning back for Mary, Jeff and their now complete marriage. They were very happy together. There were no plans for more children; they thought themselves very lucky, after everything they had gone through, to have Barry. If another did come along well that would be fine as well.

CHAPTER TWO:
Close Encounters of the Strange Kind.

[Back with Neil in Scarborough; it is now late September 1963]

'It's time for another early morning jog along the beach' Neil decided, kicking off his slippers, tying up his plimsolls and heading for the door. 'At least the weather is a little better today,' he decided as he stuck his head outside. The last few days had been pretty poor. Back to full health, physically and in a better place emotionally, Neil had still kept up most of his exercise routine and in particular his regular run along the beach.

He would sometimes vary the direction of his run so that he would not get bored with it. On occasions, he would add a new obstacle like taking the steps near to St Nicholas Cliff usually going down or if he was feeling very energetic he would climb them towards the end of his run and enter Eastborough from the opposite direction. If the tide was in he would stick to the pavements and now and then even run along Marine Drive which connects the South and North Bays.

Today he decided to keep to his normal route. 'I wonder if I will see her again?' he thought, as he stepped outside and locked the door of his flat. This time his mind was not on Fiona. That was a good thing. He would never forget her, but for his own sanity, he had to start to concern himself with the present and look to the future.

When he thought 'I wonder if I will see her again?' he was referring to the strange encounter he had the other day. Having run on the same stretch of beach many times in the early morning, Neil knew just about every face and every dog he encountered at that time of day. You could even say he knew every pebble, but that might be taking it a bit too far.

Also having previously visited the area, during late September, he knew it was used mainly by the locals at this time of year. Even the most popular beaches were used less and less by holidaymakers as the season started to draw to a close and anyway before 8.00a.m., encounters were few and far between. He was often in a world all of his own and although he recognised people that he had seen before he rarely stopped to talk, just a nod of the head or a wave of the hand. However two days ago he had noticed a very smart yet unfamiliar lady on his stretch of beach. Actually, that last sentence does not do any justice to the very strange encounter that had occurred.

[Two days earlier]

It wasn't just that he had never seen her there before it was also the very strange way the meeting unfolded. He had slowed down a lot as he was nearing the end of his run and almost back to his favourite resting place. He stopped for a while to admire the scenery. The sky was unusually beautiful that morning. The cloud made unusual trails and the early morning sky was an orangey red where it touched the sea on the horizon.

He was just about to continue when he became aware that he was being looked at. Not just watched but looked at in what seemed like an inquisitive piercing sort of way. She wore smart clothing and Neil thought that slightly odd. She did not seem dressed for the beach or for jogging and therefore looked a little out of place. She moved nearer to him and as if on purpose, changed her original path, seemingly to get a closer look. She stopped walking just a yard away from Neil, stood in front of him, and stared directly into his eyes. The two now stood motionless looking at each other.

"Do I know you?" said Neil thinking her actions very strange and feeling rather uncomfortable.

"No!" she said, and as if to suddenly realise what she had been doing apologised, *"Sorry!"* and again, *"Sorry..."* Naturally, feeling rather embarrassed she continued, *"I, I thought you were someone I knew,"* then blushed and ran off. She then felt even more embarrassed when she looked back and noticed Neil had also turned to get another look at her.

That was strange, thought Neil. He meant because of what had happened but perhaps more so because he had this odd feeling inside him. All he could think was 'I want to see her again.' This encounter had sparked something inside that made him want to know more about her. He did not have a clue why. It wasn't about fancying her. Meeting someone new was far from his mind and as far as girls were concerned he had more or less kept himself to himself since waking from his coma. She was quite good looking but his first impressions saw very little to write home about. He did, however, notice two things that stood out as plus points. **[No not those]**. It was her eyes, he thought, 'big, brown and beautiful.'

This strange encounter seemed to have taken over his thoughts. 'This is silly' he decided and dismissed her from his mind.

Well, he tried to dismiss her, but his mind kept returning him to the moment they met almost face to face. This was followed by this unexplained urge to get to know her.

[Back trying to think about the present]

As he ran passed the Life Boat Station and on to the beach he found himself actively looking to see her again. He kept running along the sand, as was the norm, away from the harbour end of the beach. He was on his normal route yet things did not seem normal. He was much more aware today of what was going on around him. It was not just his legs that were running because 'she' kept running through his mind. He asked himself 'what is this madness that possesses me?' as he turned to run back again and all this time remaining 'eyes peeled.' Twenty minutes later he was almost back to his starting point and sitting on the wall where he often rested. Neil scanned the horizon. This time, not to admire the scenery, but with his eyes trained to look for people. Well, not just any people, but one particular person, the stranger on the shore.

It was good to rest. His run was exhilarating and he knew it was doing him the world of good but it was so good to rest. All was now calm.

His heartbeat and breathing had returned to normal and all was quite peaceful. Peaceful that is apart from the sounds he was accustomed to, the traffic behind him, the seagulls above him and the sea waves crashing in front of him a couple of hundred yards away.

Then, without a word of warning, a loud voice…

"Nice day!" and a hand on his shoulder. The voice and hand came from behind him emanating from the other side of the wall. The stranger had got over her embarrassment from their last encounter and had bucked up enough courage to, once more, approach Neil.

"Yes" replied a shocked Neil almost jumping as he turned to speak *"It's a……,"* he stopped speaking, his tongue starting to fail him, as he realised who it was. *"Won…der…ful day,"* he managed to finish his sentence. His reaction was partly due to the sudden and unexpected interruption, but also because it was **her**. He was again filled with that strange feeling and his thought was, 'I so want to get to know you.'

She then explained. *"Look, I just wanted to apologise properly for the other day."*

Stuck for words, unlike the day before yesterday, it was now Neil's turn to feel embarrassed. *"Err, well um, hum,"* was his less than intelligent reply as he stood up to face her. Well, they did not manage face to face as the sands were much lower than the pavement and she was standing at the other side of the wall. It was more like his face to her navel.

"You must have thought me very peculiar but I honestly thought you were someone I had met before."

Finally after what seemed like an age of just looking up and down at each other Neil pulled himself together and said, *"That's OK! Think nothing of it!"* Knowing **he** had done nothing but **think** of it since it happened. Reaching up and holding out his right hand towards her over the wall where he had been sitting, *"Neil, Neil Collins,"* he said, introducing himself.

"Helen Crosby," she said. Bending her knees and her back slightly she reached down and shook his hand, gently but firmly, feeling pleased that his reaction was friendly. Another seemingly long pause followed, ending in both trying to speak at the same time.

"Are you on hol...?" Neil started to say.
"Do you live...?" Helen stopped speaking to allow Neil to continue.

"It's a little awkward," said Neil, referring to having to look up at her from the beach.

Helen knew what he was referring to *"Yes you may get a crick in your neck like that,"* she agreed. *"Let's walk on, to the end of the wall."* She pointed as she made the suggestion. At that, they both set off towards the Lifeboat Station. Reaching the end of the wall, Neil joined her on the pavement and they were now, at last, on the same level. *"You were about to ask me something?"* reminded Helen.

"I was just wondering. Are you on holiday?" He asked, starting where he had left off.

"No actually I have just moved here away from the big city," answered Helen. *"And you?"*

"I have lived here for over a year now."

"Where did you use to live?" Helen asked.

"Northallerton," he replied.

"I used to know someone who lived in Northallerton, what street did you live in?"

"Quaker Lane," was the reply.

"What brings you here then?" She questioned further and went on to ask several more quite probing questions.

Not really wanting to give much away to someone who seemed quite a nice person but was a stranger, Neil stopped her in mid-flow and brought a halt to her grilling. While he would have liked to find out more about **her**, he started to feel a little uncomfortable and did not really feel like sharing **his** life story with someone he had only known for a few minutes.

"Look I, I'd better go – I have been out quite some time and I have things that need my attention," he said, trying not to offend but at the same time, being firm.

"Yes, sure," Helen said and added, *"I understand."* With that, Neil sped off running quite fast for the first fifty yards across Foreshore Road and kept running for a little way up the bank towards home. This was more of a sprint than a jog and not his normal slow walk for the last bit of his morning exercise.

"Bye," she shouted. He had already started running.

"Bye," he briefly half turned, once he had safely crossed the road and waved.

It almost appeared that she had been giving him the third degree. 'I wonder why?' he thought, 'this was more than just for the sake of conversation, it was a second rather strange encounter. Perhaps she was nervous and could not think of anything else to say.' He seemed to be coming to her defence but soon turned his attention to the work-a-day jobs waiting for him back home.

He had not done any paid work since before the accident. Most of the time he could not but he was now thinking of doing something to fill in his days and to support himself financially. He had been living off the compensation, car insurance and Fiona's life cover he received, but that was not going to last a lifetime - far from it. So he needed to find some work, hopefully, something he could enjoy that would pay well.

[Later that day]

"Oh yes! Window cleaning day today." He said out loud as if to jolt himself into action and jumped up off the chair. There really was no special day for window cleaning. Neil is a man, in other words, window cleaning, or for that matter, any other household chore is not a priority. That does not mean he did not keep the flat clean. He certainly did, but he was not fastidious. After switching on the wireless for 'Music While You Work' he grabbed the appropriate cleaning materials, a bucket of hot water, a chamois leather, a drying cloth, some detergent and made a start. It was just the inside of the windows, he paid someone to clean the outside once a fortnight. Even that did not seem enough. Having a busy road outside meant the windows got pretty mucky, pretty quickly and were not a pretty sight. When the time came around the window cleaner certainly earned his money. It must have been, maybe, six months ago or more since the insides were last cleaned.

As 'Calling All Workers' the signature tune to 'Music While You Work[4]' filled the air from his wireless he jokingly thought 'If I move my cloth to the tempo of this tune and the others that follow I will get the windows done more quickly.'

He was naturally looking at the glass and not completely aware of what was going on in the street. He bent down to his bucket, to replenish the soap suds. Turning back to the window he happened to glance outside and he could not believe his eyes. It was Helen, Helen Crosby, looking for the briefest of moments straight and directly at him from the other side of the road. As soon as she realised she had been spotted she turned and pretended to be looking into the shop window, the one that had been directly behind her. This pretence was obvious to Neil. What Helen was not aware of immediately was that she was now window shopping at the local funeral parlour.

Realising the silliness of what she was pretending to do she sidled sheepishly to the right ending up outside the next shop. 'Thank goodness, a cake shop' she thought trying to convince herself she had not been noticed or at least did not look as if she was spying on Neil. After surveying the window, unconvincingly, she thought 'I had better go in and buy something.'

'Is she stalking me?' Neil wondered 'She must have followed me because I did not mention my new address here in Scarborough. It seemed too much of a coincidence that she should now be 'shopping' in Eastborough after having looked directly into my window.' Wondering what to do next he temporarily cleaned the same section of window vigorously two or three times. He was now looking, with great difficulty, through ever-increasing mountains of bubbles. He wiped away the bubbles from a portion of the window to enable him to see across the street to where he last noticed her disappear into the cake shop. After about five minutes of creating loads of foamy soap suds, with still no sign of her, he could no longer control his urge to go in pursuit.

Dropping everything, to find out what was going on, he dashed straight outside. Sleeves still rolled up he entered the cake shop with soap suds just about everywhere. He looked around but no Helen to be found.

The shop assistant looked at him thinking 'what on earth?' and said, *"Can I help you sir?"* wondering who in their right mind would come shopping for cakes looking as if he had just got out of the bath.

At that point, Neil apologised realising he was carrying half the soap suds with him not just on his arms but all over the front of his shirt and his shoulders finally forming a halo around his head.

"Just cleaning the windows," not knowing what else to say or what other explanation would make sense.

As Neil left the shop the assistant looked at the shop windows then looked at another customer, circled a finger near to her temple, shrugged her shoulders, shook her head and got back to the job of serving, muttering, *"Barmy bugger!,"* under her breath so the customers could not hear her.

'I can only think one of two things' Neil said to himself. 'Either she coincidentally left the shop during the few seconds it took me to make my way outside, or the vapour from that window cleaning fluid is stronger than I thought. 'Was it all imagined?'

He settled for his first idea, shrugged his shoulders and went back to his window cleaning albeit a little bit distracted.

[The next day]

When he awoke the next morning and opened the curtains he found himself scanning the street for any signs of a stalker. 'This is silly' he decided and got on with his day, nipping out for a paper.

He trawled through the jobs page, as he ate his breakfast, then set to writing a few letters to the companies that seemed to have something in his line of work. 'Mechanics jobs or perhaps manufacturing or something in engineering,' he mulled over in his mind. 'probably anything involving working with my hands or tools' He decided would be best yet at the moment he would likely settle for just about anything.

Sealing the envelopes he was off out to the post office. Having purchased and stuck on the stamps he dropped the application letters into the box and made his way towards the exit. 'Please God,' he said a silent prayer, 'let something good come from at least one of my letters.'

As he came out of the post office he caught sight of Helen on the top deck of a bus. **'Right!'** he thought 'I am going to get to the bottom of this' and ran like the wind managing, just about, to keep up with the bus. Brushing aside one or two innocent bystanders he jumped aboard at the next stop.

"Where are you going?" he was immediately confronted by the conductor.

"Upstairs," a shocked, surprised and slightly breathless Neil replied, not really thinking about the question. It wasn't an unfit type of breathlessness more anxious excitement.

One would be quite surprised that Neil was quite surprised, as if getting on a bus did not normally require you to know where you wanted to go. He was also surprised at being confronted by the conductor as soon as he jumped on board. He did not realise that the conductor was just trying to save his own legs. He had collected all the fares upstairs already.

Also, Neil's mind was only on one thing – catching up with Helen.

The conductor threw his head back and went *"Tuch!"* making that almost clicking noise with his tongue against the roof of his mouth and rolling his eyes dismissively as if to say 'we have a right Charlie here,' and went on to say *"No I mean where are you **travelling** to?"* Now the conductor was becoming a little impatient.

"Err, well, I, I........don't know," and while searching for some change added, *"Where does this bus go?"* realising he had no small change just a ten shilling note[5].

"All the way to the terminus," the conductor said as if now, washing his hands of him.

"The terminus then please," requested Neil. Quickly pressing the ten shilling note into the conductor's hand, he grabbed the ticket and shot upstairs.

"Here you are, Sir." The conductor tried, in vain, to catch Neil's attention and stop him going upstairs without his change. He was holding out his hand towards him, along with a substantial amount of money, but Neil had no knowledge of the conductor's efforts. He was so determined to complete his 007 like mission which was to apprehend and grill Helen for the truth. 'Give her the third degree' he decided 'even more of a grilling than she tried to give me.' I am sure if he had a torch with him he would have wanted to shine it into her eyes.

The conductor, stared at the money in his hand, looked all around, 'did anyone see that?' he asked himself and quickly put Neil's change into his own pocket. Shrugging his shoulders and whistling a tune with a smug semi-smile on his face he was off to collect the fares on the lower deck.

Turning the tables on Helen for coming up behind and surprising him at the beach Neil's sudden appearance beside her caused quite a shock. She was so shocked it was almost as if she had been struck dumb.

"Well, what is this all about?" demanded Neil after plonking himself down beside her, with an air of determination. He knew that she knew exactly what he was referring to.

Helen looked at him, opened her mouth but nothing came out.

Neil put it to her ***"Are you stalking me?"***

Finally, Helen, pulling herself together, went on the attack and asked *"Are **you** stalking **me**? I am on the way to town and it is you who have approached me."*
"Well that was coincidence," objected Neil. *"I was busy doing something else when I just happened to notice you on this bus, so jumped on board."* He then added very firmly ***"What about yesterday?"*** bringing the subject of the conversation back to *her* and *her* actions, not his.

*"Could **that** not have been a coincidence?"* she pleaded, realising she had given the weakest of defences and even as she asked did not expect it to be taken as an acceptable explanation. To a certain degree, she was telling the truth. She had followed Neil from the beach but he was so far ahead she had only caught a glimpse of him vanishing into a doorway. She had no idea which doorway just the area of Eastborough in which he had disappeared. Knowing she had to go shopping that day and that finding him could prove to be a big job, she decided to put it off till later when the shops were open and when there would be more people available to ask.

Arriving back in Eastborough and still not knowing how best to find Neil's front door Helen walked aimlessly up and down on the opposite side of the road. Staring across the road into each window she was beginning to think it a lost cause when, *coincidentally,* Neil looked out of the very window she was looking into. She explained and apologised. *"I hope you will forgive me and that we can be friends."*

"With the best will in the world I cannot really accept your apology or your explanation," answered Neil in a matter of fact way.

"Why?" She looked at him pleadingly.

"Because it still doesn't tell me why you did it," said Neil in quite an exasperated tone of voice.

"It looks like I am going to have to tell you the truth doesn't it?" Helen said in her most honest and convincing voice.

"Well I think that would be the best thing," Neil said, thinking 'what, I wonder, will she come up with next?'

She turned directly towards him, looked him straight in the eyes, and admitted. *"I like you..."* paused a moment then added *"... I like you very much."* She then paused for a second time to take in the look on Neil's stern face which immediately started to soften. 'Keep going' she thought to herself, feeling a lump starting to form in her throat. 'You're doing OK,' and went on *"I liked you from the first moment we met and I wanted to make sure I saw you again,"* she said as she used her finger to wipe away the first sign of a tear from her eye. She continued, *"You ran off before I was able to find out your address so I had to follow you which took some doing I can tell you. You didn't half run fast."* Then, she added, in a surprised tone, *"And uphill!"*

Neil was stunned. He was certainly not expecting that. He really did not know what to say or how to react. He felt quite flattered actually. I don't mean when she referred to his running ability, I mean the bit about her liking him. It did a lot for his self-esteem. He had not had many compliments lately and certainly not much contact with the fairer sex.

As he wondered how to reply he looked at Helen and realised then that, despite her efforts, a tear had spilt over the corner of her eye. He felt, rightly or wrongly that she was being honest. This adding to his inner feeling of being drawn towards her made him feel some sympathy.

"Please, don't cry," Neil said softly and offered her his clean handkerchief. Thanks to his lovely Aunty Annie he was taught always to carry a clean handkerchief with him. It was certainly useful today. He suggested, *"Let's go and have a cuppa"* and with that, they decided to get off the bus near to the town centre. There was a very good Italian style cafe, not far from the bus stop, called Spinetti's. *"They serve excellent frothy coffee,"* said Neil trying to lighten the atmosphere.

"That sounds good. I do like my frothy coffee," pronounced Helen.

As they got to the bottom of the steps which lead from the upper to lower decks of the bus the conductor gave Neil a rather odd looking satisfied grin, more of a wry smile and winked. 'What's got into him' Neil thought as he stepped off the bus took three strides and stopped dead in his tracks.

"My change!" he suddenly realised, trying to follow the bus, but it was too late the bus, and his change, sped off down the street.

"What's the matter?" asked Helen.

"Oh it's nothing," answered Neil, realising he had more important things to attend to at the present.

Luigi Spinetti was a lovable gentle giant. The elderly Italian cafe owner stood like a monolith, behind his counter or anywhere else he chose to stand. He was a very tall and very wide monolith at that. Sporting a moustache and usually friendly smile he wore a type of chef's uniform.

It was made up of blue checked trousers and a dazzling white tunic, along with a flat chef's hat. This was also white and sat at a jaunty angle slightly to one side of his partly balding head. Luigi completed his ensemble with a blue checked scarf that matched his trousers.

Yes, he was a huge man, but normally very likeable because of his friendliness to the customers and spoke with a distinct Italian accent. Well he would, wouldn't he?

It was good that he was as tall as he was wide because, despite his normally pleasant personality, it helped him to sort out problem customers when he needed to. His enormity enabled him to deal, sternly, strictly and sometimes very forcibly with some of the more troublesome 'Rockers' or perhaps the odd unruly 'Teddy-Boy.' People liked Spinetti's for that very reason; there was less chance of encountering any yobbish behaviour while enjoying your refreshments, chatting with friends or listening to the jukebox. Any disturbances were very quickly dealt with. There had been a few heads knocked together in the past.

Luigi always had a smile for his patrons. I am sure he was sincere even though his smile seemed to get bigger the more money customers were spending.

Neil placed their order, *"Two frothy coffees please Luigi."*

"Yes-a Sir," Luigi said politely.

Neil and Helen had a good long chat over a couple of the best frothy coffees in town. As they sat talking someone chose a record from the jukebox. Yes you guessed it. Those wonderful melodic tones of Acker Bilks full-bodied clarinet rang out from the speakers.

"They are playing your song," suggested Neil to Helen.

At first, she looked bewildered but quickly realised the title 'Stranger on the Shore.'

"Oh! Yes," she said and suggested, *"Well, let's say **our** song, shall we?"* Then added, *"Remember you are, sorry, you **were** also a stranger to me."* Neil nodded in agreement and they smiled at each other.

Helen convinced him there was nothing sinister about her trying to keep tabs on him. As they spoke those feelings he had about her, those unexplainable feelings of needing to know more about this stranger returned and to a certain extent were fulfilled. He felt that he knew more about her now and what he learned he liked. What he saw in front of him he liked. He found Helen to be a slim articulate woman in the prime of her life. She was witty, intelligent and engaging. Neil again could not help but notice her eyes, big, brown and beautiful, with long eyelashes. These were real eyelashes, eyelashes that many women would be very jealous of.

Evidently, she was married but waiting for the divorce papers to come through. Sadly her son had died young. When she spoke of this she became emotional and did not want to talk about it anymore. Neil respected that. He was very sympathetic; after all, he had had lots of experience losing people very close to him, he knew just how traumatic it was. So he did care very much about her loss and was going to ask what happened, her son's name, how he died, and perhaps how old he was. However, Neil could see Helen was hurting so did not pursue it further. He realised just how upsetting it was for her to talk about and decided against any further reference to the matter.

Turning once more to her story, and changing the subject Neil said, *"What do you do for a living then?"*

"Well - nothing at the moment," returned Helen and added, *"I went to university and gained a degree. The idea was that I would join my father's company on the business and accounting side, but that has not happened yet. What about you?"*

"I am a mechanic by trade. I started as an apprentice at Smurthwaite's garage in Northallerton just after I left school. I am out of work at the moment but I'm sure I will find something given time."

Most of the chat was now just small talk, but they seemed to be enjoying each other's company. In fact, you will still find them sitting talking and drinking coffee at the start of chapter five.

[We will, for a short while, leave our friends enjoying each other's company while I tell you more about Neil's life with Fiona, how they met and their very special love. As with most of the story this will be mainly seen through Neil's eyes. It is a very important part of the story because it will supply you with the background information that will help you to understand the reasons for his actions and reactions to future events. We meet up with him on the second anniversary of Fiona's death on another of his early morning exercise runs on Scarborough beach. As this special day unfolds we will be transported via Neil's mind and be allowed to witness some of Neil's fondest memories of his time with Fiona. We will also share some of their precious moments and get to know a lot more about their relationship.]

CHAPTER THREE: Precious Moments.

[Neil, out jogging again 9th August 1963]

Knowing this was a big day, and that he had a lot to do, he set out earlier than usual this morning. His jogging seemed heavy going today which may have had something to do with the fact that it was the second anniversary of the accident. Never a day had gone past without his thoughts turning to the love he had lost so cruelly. After his shorter than usual exercise period, he decided to sit and rest for a while, in his usual place, as he had often done before. Despite his efforts to avert his mind from the sad memories he just, at that moment, became overwhelmed with grief.

His emotions started to get the better of him, and he cried out softly to the heavens mouthing, **"Why? Oh! Why?"** The tears cascaded down his face. He was looking up to heaven as if speaking to God in wretched desperation. Even though he knew it could never happen he wished Fiona could be back with him again. He felt it was a great injustice to him to have lost her. Injustice also to her, that one so young, so good and so beautiful should have her life cut, so short. He sat there and rested for longer than usual. Not to recover from his exercise but in his attempt to recover his composure. Eventually, he dried his eyes and started to feel better. After allowing those pent up emotions to be released through the safety valve of human emotion he was able to continue. He left the beach but was not ready to go home yet. He knew he would be calling in at the shops and wanted to be sure he had pulled himself together properly before he got there, so he found himself meandering a little taking in streets that were new to him.

His longer route than usual took him within earshot of the Friarage Community Primary School he only became aware of that when he realised he could hear the sound of children's voices emanating from the playground.

It was a chorus; yes almost a choir of cheery voices but without a conductor. Quite what the words were was impossible to know. Perhaps it was just the joy of being alive and being so young. They sounded as if they were singing from the same song sheet yet each child's part was different from the next. This regular noise was, from time to time, out sung by one or two soloists hitting the highest or loudest of notes.

Neil was somehow drawn to the noise and ended up in Longwestgate. The choir was hushed by the sound of a ringing bell although some wayward choristers insisted on singing another verse whilst lining up to go into school.

'Those were the days' he said to himself as he started to recall the day he first met Fiona. He stopped walking as the memories of his school days, in Northallerton, came flooding back.

[Neil and Fiona's first meeting as childhood sweethearts 1952]

"Come on get up, you're going to be late if you don't come down now," shouted Aunty Annie from the bottom of the stairs.

"I am up!" Neil replied quite impudently.

"I hope you have your vest on," Aunty Annie reminded him knowing he would sometimes carelessly leave it off or he would take it off too soon before the good weather had properly arrived. 'Cast ye no clout till May is out' she thought 'I keep telling him that.'

"Yes I've got my vest on," was the reply. 'Well I have now' he thought, as he quickly whipped his shirt back off, pulled the vest from under his pile of clothes and put it on.

"And your breakfast is getting cold, you don't want to be late on your last day," came another shout from below.

"Ok Aunty Annie, I'm ready now," assured Neil, the fifteen-year-old schoolboy, and within a second or two dashed out of his room and **thumped** down the stairs. Like most children do, he made more noise than ten full-grown men twice his size.

Realising he was late he stood at the table to gulp some tea. Then, almost at a run, went around the kitchen grabbed a slice of toast, picked up his school bag and planted a kiss on Aunty Annie's face. After taking a large bite of delicious very buttery toast, his sister Jenny's face got the same kissing treatment. Whilst he loved his sister, Neil had planted the kiss more as a joke, leaving as a parting gift, a large smattering of butter and lots of crumbs on her cheek and ran out of the kitchen.

"Aaarrgh... Neil!" protested Jenny as she immediately tried to rub the mess off with the back of her hand.

"What a cheeky boy," commented Aunty Annie, and shouted after him, **"It's raining, you had better put your raincoat on,"** On impulse, he ignored her and, ran straight out of the front door, still chewing on his toast.

Neil was normally quite a calm studious boy but once in a blue moon would do something impulsive. He would carry this contradictive personality trait with him into adulthood. Thankfully he also carried lots of the good things his aunt had taught him.

It was a particularly wet day with puddles lying just about everywhere and the rain still pouring down. 'Wish I had brought my raincoat' he decided. He was running late again and this was his last day at the Allertonshire County Modern School.

He ran down Brompton Road and headed for the school. Dashing around a corner near to the school playground, he ran straight into her, almost knocking her off her feet. Although he did not know it at the time, 'her' was his future wife, Fiona.

"Aaaugh!" shouted Fiona, as she and her pile of books along with other items for school use, were sent flying by this out of control boy. She steadied herself against the school wall and looked unbelievingly, first at Neil, then at her scattered belongings and back to Neil.

He had no idea why she was carrying all this equipment and books, perhaps her satchel was full. Her journey was made even more difficult because one of her hands was being used to hold up her umbrella.

Neil stopped running. Well you would! Although slightly younger she was almost as tall as Neil and hitting her square on with her load of books, had a certain similarity to hitting a brick wall. He just managed to escape having an eye put out by one of the spiky bits of her umbrella. I think we all know what that feels like.

He then started helping her to pick up everything off the wet and in parts muddy pavement. *"So sorry,"* he murmured and repeated, *"So sorry,"* several times.

"Oh that's wonderful," she said sarcastically, again looking around at the mayhem he had caused, and not knowing where or how to salvage things. One of her books was virtually destroyed. It was so wet the writing on the pages of her essay, which had to be handed in that day, were all smudged and some were dropping out as she held it up between her fingertips. *"Just look at this,"* she voiced her disgust at the state of it.

After everything he had done to this, now bedraggled, young girl Neil felt guilty and very embarrassed for several reasons. First obviously for the chaos he had just caused. Second, he knew he was late and could not stick around too long apologising or helping her to pick the multitude of items off the ground. Finally and most importantly she was the girl of his dreams.

He had been longing to meet her and had never thought it would happen. He admired her from afar and after spending the last year trying to pluck up the courage to say hello he had just come closer to her, although just for the briefest of moments than he could ever imagine he would. 'How embarrassing,' he thought as he kept trying in vain to right the wrong.

"I'm so sorry," he repeated as he picked up the last pen and ruler and handed it to her.

"Is that all you have to say?" Fiona asked.

*"Well I am **really** sorry, I will replace anything broken, I promise, but I really have to go now or I'll be late."* With that, he was off like a shot into the school entrance and through the main doors just as the final bell could be heard.

She too followed very closely behind as she also would be late if she did not hurry. 'That is all I needed,' she thought, 'bumping into some idiot boy.'

Neil was so distracted by the events of that morning and very excited about actually having been standing next to and talking to Fiona that he found it difficult to think about anything else. It is just as well it was his last day at school as learning was far from his thoughts. He just wished his meeting had been in different circumstances. 'My chances with Fiona are now less than zero' he decided.

The fifteen-year-old, love-struck, Neil was a very different boy from the one that, at the age of twelve, started Allertonshire County Modern School. Like most twelve-year-old boys he agreed with his mates that playing or associating with girls is sissy and that 'girls are wimps'. Not that he repeated that phrase in front of his sister Jenny, who he had enjoyed growing up with. He had happy memories of playing many different games such as top and whip and cowboys and Indians. Jenny usually always ended up being the Indian squaw.

Jenny also enjoyed childhood games, except on one occasion. Once when Neil's friend Dave came over, as cowboys, they both tied the captured squaw to a lamp post, which doubled as a totem pole and left her there for half an hour while they went off and played marbles. Not very nice I know but they were only children, Neil being about eleven years of age at the time. Dave used to live next door to Neil's old house in Middlesbrough and was nearly killed by the same bomb that killed Neil's mother.

There were other children leaving school that same day. Luckily for Neil, the teachers had not arranged any special lessons which required a lot of concentration. This was a time mostly for discussions about the big wide world they were all about to be let loose into and tips on finding work or going on to college which some of them did. Luckily for Neil, a friend of a friend of Aunty Annie's put in a good word for him at Smurthwaite's Garage where he secured an apprenticeship.

The day rolled on and soon there came another playtime. This was his last playtime and he joined in a game of cricket as he usually did, using a chalked-in set of cricket stumps on the school wall.

"It's my turn to bat now," insisted Neil.

The bat was a proper cricket bat but for safety, they used a tennis ball. If they had used a cricket ball they would have been counting the dead and injured each day. Most of the victims were not playtime cricketers but those who simply happened to be near when the batsman tried for a 'four' or a 'six'. When any child was hit by the ball it could still sting quite badly, especially if it was on the skin, but at least they lived to tell the tale.

Neil was usually pretty good at batting. So far he had scored three legs, two backs, one bum, an elbow and a bloody nose. As well as scoring a few runs.

"Ouzat!" shouted the little boy with the freckled face. He managed to grab the ball out of the sky from a shot that was going over his head. Despite his height, he proved he could jump and with one hand brought the ball under his control.

"Well caught," a shout of congratulations came from one of freckleface's friends and Neil was out for twelve runs.

'Not the best of innings' he thought, 'quite a disaster really,' as he handed his bat to the next person in line. 'Then again,' he decided, 'not quite as much of a disaster as this morning when I bowled a maiden over.' Whilst he had allowed himself to make a joke he could not even manage a quiet chuckle because of the sadness he felt about messing up.

Shortly after his innings, he was still in the playground leaning against the wall watching the 'Ashes' match being played out when 'Oh no' he moaned under his breath. Fiona was heading towards him. He would normally have been very pleased that his dream girl was heading his way but under the present circumstances, and by her demeanour, he was not looking forward to this encounter. The last encounter was still fresh on his mind and no doubt on hers as well.

"Hey you boy!" she shouted, ***"I want a word in your ear."***

After all this time of imagining what it would be like to get to know her, just at that moment, he felt she was the last person on earth he wanted walking towards him, especially, having seen that steely look in her eyes. She came directly towards him, a grim determination on her face and an ever more meaningful stride as she got closer.

Neil pulled himself up to his full height raised one hand out in front of him as if in defence of what he thought was about to happen and said in a very apologetic tone.

"I know I have already apologised but, I really...."

Fiona interrupted him, saying in a very stern and commanding voice, ***"I have something to say to you!"***

Neil stood his ground, waiting for the punch line or perhaps even the punch. He was never one for getting into fights and certainly not with a girl and definitely not with his dream girl. At the age of thirteen, Fiona was, as you know, a little smaller in stature than Neil, but she was very self-assured. Like most girls she started to mature earlier than her male counterparts and seemed, certainly by this encounter, to be very confident.

There was silence which seemed to go on forever but was probably just a few seconds as they eyed each other up. The tension was building and he was just about to speak when Fiona broke the silence, aggressively, almost shouting. She leaned very close to him in a menacing way.

"I just wanted to say...," she paused and as she did so, relaxed her posture. A sweet smile lit up her face and in her most charming voice, she said, *"thank you,"* with a twinkle in her eyes.

"What!" Neil blurted out sounding quite ungrateful. He did not mean to sound like that and quickly said, *"I mean why?"* and added, *"I'm shocked."*

"Well I had not completed the essay that you ruined and I was able to use the mishap as an excuse for not handing it in. I would have been in real trouble if it had gone in unfinished," concluded Fiona.

It was as if a huge heavy stone had been lifted from Neil's shoulders. He relaxed his defensive mode and a broad smile spread across his face.

"Well that is good news," announced Neil thinking more about his own saving grace rather than hers. Realising he was being a little selfish he added: *"I am really pleased everything has turned out..."* Neil stopped mid-sentence and the smile on his face disappeared being replaced with incredulity, "**Hey....just a minute!** *What was all this threatening behaviour, angry looks and shouting just a moment ago?"*

"Well, I didn't want to let you off completely scot-free did I?" answered Fiona, winking knowingly, *"I thought you deserved a **little** punishment,"* pulling gently on his tie.

Thinking about it Neil saw the funny side and they both started to laugh out loud. Suddenly without warning, in the midst of all the laughter, they grasped each other spontaneously. An inner feeling of relief, that all was well with the world, ran through their bodies. A cuddle and a bit of excited jumping up and down and round about seemed the appropriate celebration for two youngsters. It was an outward, expression of their inner feeling. They almost immediately released each other as they realised what they were doing. They stopped laughing and stepped back. After all, it was a little early for **touching** as they had more or less just met.

A sort of embarrassing moment passed with no conversation. Red faces appeared as they both felt a mixture of, how did that happen, wish I hadn't done that, glad I did, would like to do it again, flowed through their veins.

Eventually, Neil stuttered, *"R, R, Right... well... umm... I... I... will..."*

"See you later?" Fiona said questioningly, finishing his sentence, and they turned to go their separate ways.

Neil realised this could be the last time he ever saw her, 'A' because he was leaving school today and 'B' he did not know her name. 'Come on' he thought 'pull yourself together' and with that, he ran back and tapped her on the shoulder. She turned but did not have time to say anything...

"Do you like roller skating?" Neil asked.

"Well I don't know I have never been," she answered.

"Would you like to come with me to the South Park in Darlington on Saturday?" Neil said enthusiastically.

"*Yes please,*" she replied equally enthusiastically, "*as long as you hold me up.*" They both laughed.

"*You know - I don't even know your name,*" Neil said sounding surprised. They swapped names and had a short discussion about where to meet and at what time.

Fiona was fair-haired, almost blonde, and her eyes were a wonderful shade of blue with a twinkle in them that she seemed to be able to turn on whenever the need arose.
She was a good looking girl Neil had no doubt about that. It was her beauty that first caught his eye just over a year ago. During the days, weeks and months of their future teenage courtship, he found that she was just as beautiful inside as she was on the outside and that the anger shown towards him earlier had all been an act.

She was not very pleased at first at being nearly knocked over and having all her books etc thrown on the muddy, wet pavement. However, the threatening behaviour and raised voices were just a little ploy to get her own back on this tearaway who she had taken an immediate dislike to. It was the sudden urge to grab him in celebration, though brief, which was enough for her to know that there was something special about Neil. Later she reflected 'I am so glad he chased after me and asked me for a date.'

It was quite a long bus ride to Darlington. They stayed on the bus to the station, decided to look around the town centre shops. They then had a fair walk to the South Park via Victoria Embankment which runs along by the River Skerne. As they reached the park gates and stopped to buy ice creams, from the little mobile kiosk, they could hear the music ringing out from the loudspeakers at the skating rink. It was mostly 78r.p.m. recordings by Don Mackay, playing roller dance music on the Hammond organ, interspersed with one or two popular tunes of the day by people like Johnnie Ray singing 'Walking my baby back home.' Neil could skate but he was not as good as those who took every opportunity to dance to the strict tempo organ music. He was amazed at the way they moved quickly and effortlessly in time to the music across the rink, sometimes as couples, carrying out some very clever footwork. 'They are even turning from forwards to backwards and back again on one foot' he thought in amazement.

They really enjoyed their skating. Neil and Fiona had a great time on their first date. Fiona was a little unsteady at first but soon got used to balancing on eight wheels. She did a lot better than most and within half an hour could skate on her own reasonably safely. Never-the-less she still held tightly on to Neil's hand for most of the rest of the day, even off the skating rink.

[His thoughts came back to the present 9th August 1963]

Having now fully taken control of his emotions he focused on the need to buy some flowers and decided 'First I'll call into the local newsagents and buy a paper.'

"Hello Neil!" said John the shop owner a little surprised. *"You're early today,"* came his upbeat greeting.

"Yes, I am going to visit my wife's grave so I need time to travel to Northallerton.

"Oh... of course..." His wide smile contracted. *"It's her anniversary isn't it?"* said John. This time, in a thoughtful caring voice, realising it wasn't a time for quite such an up-tempo demeanour.

"Yeh," Neil replied, picking up a paper from the shelf. A few months ago, on a rather slow customer day, John had kept Neil talking a lot more than usual and had asked him a lot of questions. Not in a nosy parker way, but in a sincere and sympathetic way, revealing much of Neil's past.

"How are you doing these days?" inquired John. Finding the right words was difficult.

"Oh! I'm fine," answered Neil, not really knowing what to say next, remembering it was only half an hour ago he was in pieces. Having

deflected the question he turned his attention elsewhere so as not to become emotional all over again. He happened to notice John had some flowers for sale. *"Hey, those red roses look particularly good,"* commented Neil. *"Is this a new line?"*

"Yes," replied John, *"I am trying it out to see how it goes."*

"That is fortunate, they are just what I need," said Neil. He then pointed to a particularly nice bunch and handing John a pound note said, *"I'll take those, please John."*

"Great, that's a Daily Express, threepence, plus nine and six for the twelve roses. So that's...nine shillings and nine pence altogether. So you want, err, ten shillings and three pence change." Neil took his change, thanked John and off he went, walking again, so as not to damage the roses and anyway 'I have done enough running for one day' he said to himself.

Back at the flat, he temporarily put the flowers in the sink covering the end of the stems in water. He showered, dressed and tried to relax with the morning paper and a cup of coffee. 'I love the smell of coffee' he mused. Neil used to drink a lot of tea and still does but the coffee, albeit instant, smelled and tasted so good he had developed a real liking for it. He remembered what was called 'Camp Coffee' that his Aunty Annie used to buy when he was a child. 'It was a liquid, I think sometimes known as chicory essence[6].' Neil seemed to remember, 'a picture on the bottle showing people camping and wearing pith helmets and safari clothes, standing near a tent,' but was not a hundred per cent sure of that.

He settled down on the couch with his mug in one hand and newspaper in the other. Despite all that had happened to Neil there were a few moments, like this one when he felt quite content. He was determined to do what Fiona would have wanted, and try to make a life for himself that was happy. Not easy but he was doing his best.

Neil normally scans the paper and only reads things that catch his eye and the headline that day was no exception. He read to himself 'There had been a mail train robbery[7], where a gang had high jacked a train containing around £2.3million, a mile from Bridego Bridge, then drove the train to the bridge to unload it.' He sipped his coffee and read on. 'The gang had Land Rovers waiting to transport the cash to a nearby hideout.'

Among the many things that caught his eye that day, towards the back of the paper, was an article on beach holidays in Spain. In the winter just gone, he had experienced one of the longest periods of bitterly cold weather he had known with ice and snow cover, not just the North of England but, over the whole country. 'Hum....a holiday in Spain' he yearned 'or somewhere else nice and warm.' That really appealed to him.

This soon set his mind wandering once again to thoughts of Fiona. He had honeymooned in Spain yet what filled his mind was a day spent, not far from Scarborough, when they were still courting. Having visited Spain he knew that neither the beaches nor the weather on the Northeast coast of England were anything like those in the Mediterranean but the day his mind transported him back to was a very special day indeed.

Putting the paper down he laid his head back on the cushion and allowed pictures of those precious moments to flood his brain.

[1957 Four years before the car crash]
School days were now long gone. Neil was twenty and Fiona in her late teens. They had been courting about five years when they decided to take a picnic to a small, isolated and usually little used beach, not far from Scarborough itself. They had come across it on one of their previous visits to Scarborough when, just for fun, they set off on an adventure of discovery.

"These sandwiches are really tasty," remarked Neil as he took another bite.

"Ham and peas pudding," replied Fiona.

"I was..." chomp, chomp *"... feeling very hungry which makes them...."* chomp chomp *".... all the more satisfying,"* said Neil feeling a little guilty for talking while eating but never-the-less he swallowed the final mouthful with relish. No, not relish as in sauce, but the enjoyment of the food, though he was not averse to a little sauciness.

Almost without pausing for breath he asked, *"Shall I open the wine?"*

"Ooo! Yes please." With that familiar twinkle in her eyes, Fiona passed him the bottle.

They had already been for a paddle. The sea was a bit too cold for a swim, yet this was one of the few days they had actually managed to visit the seaside at the same time as the weather was unusually kind and warm.

The picnic was now packed away apart from the last glass of wine...

"To us," Neil suggested a toast.

"To us," echoed Fiona as she wrapped her drinking arm around his. They each sipped the last few drops from their glass. Their focus, almost in unison, moved from glass to eye line. Looking into each other's eyes was for them, although unsaid as if they were able to see the other's innermost self and reflected back, came pure love, devotion and desire.

This closeness caused a noticeable increase in heartbeats. As they untangled their arms to dispense with the wine glasses, skin again touched skin. Neil glanced down from Fiona's beautiful blue eyes to her moist, irresistible lips from which she was now licking away the last remnants of wine. They kissed gently and lovingly yet with a passion and desire that asked for more. The kiss continued, the passion grew and the urge for more became difficult to resist.

"I think we had better stop now," remarked Fiona, unconvincingly, as she turned to put away the glasses.

"*Do you **really** mean that?*" asked Neil, provocatively, as he turned her back around to face him and slowly moved the palm of his hand across her bikini top.

Fiona naturally enjoyed the touch of Neil's hand but pressed her hand on his for him to stop. She looked all around to scan the horizon, thought for a moment, and exclaimed, "*Someone might come!*"

They looked at each other and laughed out loud when they realised that what Fiona had said could be interpreted in more ways than one.

As the laughter subsided they fell into each other's arms. Neil continued where he had left off, this time on the inside of her bikini. He then started to remove the garment and soon both knew there would be no turning back. They were adept at foreplay and knew exactly what the other enjoyed. This was not because they were very experienced lovers; on the contrary, they were each other's first and only love. They had simply learned from each other and always made every effort to please. They gave themselves willingly, unselfishly and completely.

The thrill of making love in the open air added to their delight. They could feel the gentle breeze around their, now, naked bodies. Natural loving passion together with nervous excitement that they may actually be discovered would bring them, sooner than usual, to climax.

Trying not to make a noise, "*I'm cuming,*" she whispered and her body started, involuntarily, to tense a little, as she experienced that sensational, magnificent, very pleasant feeling only a woman can relate to or begin to describe.

"*Wonderful,*" replied Neil, although he had guessed, he loved to hear her whisper that. He was now free to allow himself to orgasm. He had been trying to hold off, not really wanting the pleasure to end, but also, they always tried to make it together. They experienced that special feeling of giving and receiving that engulfs both lovers, especially when the timing is just right.

A final kiss, *"Thank you,"* Neil said sincerely. *"I love you,"* answered Fiona and both relaxed side by side. They continued to enjoy the caress of the breeze and the warmth of the sun on their skin. Love was still radiating between them like a magnetic field accompanied by a great feeling of contentment and satisfaction.

[Back at the flat 9th August 1963]

Checking the clock he realised that the time was getting on. Neil had reluctantly brought his mind back to the present. How he wished he could have Fiona back in his arms but he was very thankful for the memories. 'I had a few marvellous years with the most wonderful woman in the world,' he tried to console himself. He realised just how lucky he had been. No one else had the good fortune, love and happiness, Fiona had brought him. In his efforts to keep himself bright and cheerful he thought 'Some men have never had anyone that really loved them, never mind someone as wonderful as Fiona. Only one man in the world has had Fiona as their girlfriend, fiancé, wife and lover....that is me.'

Whilst he was sad that his future would be one without Fiona and that their time together had been so short, he realised 'we still shared an awful lot more love and happiness than some people experience over a normal lifespan' and concluded 'yes, there is always someone worse off than oneself.'

He took the last slurp of his coffee, put down his paper and almost started to nod off to sleep. Realising he felt sleepy decided to get up off the couch and headed towards the kitchen.

CHAPTER FOUR: Fond Memories.

[Still 9th August 1963]

'I had better make a move' Neil said to himself knowing he had planned to go to the cemetery, back in Northallerton, which was well over an hour away by car.

Putting the mug on the draining board he went to the cupboard for his shoes. Whilst looking in the cupboard he found their wedding album. When I say *found* I don't mean it was lost. On the contrary, it was safely stored in the cupboard in a strong, brown cardboard box. This had attracted his attention and made him instantly forget about his shoes. Well, actually he had put one shoe on and still had one foot in a slipper. He knew the album was there but it had been a long time, to save himself the heartache, since he last viewed it. Not having been married long the album had not been opened more than once or twice, since the day it was delivered from the local photographers.

'It's about time and the right time' thought Neil shuffling along, with a one-shoed foot, over to the couch where he sat back down and opened the front cover. As he did this as if by magic, music started to play. Neil wasn't dreaming or hallucinating and it wasn't violins. The album had a music box built into it and the vaguely familiar sound of Ava Maria filled the air. It was one of Fiona's favourite tunes. 'I had forgotten it played a tune' he mused 'of course I remember now.'

[Neil remembers their Wedding day on 5th April 1958]

As Neil turned the pages of the album he remembered 'What a wonderful day that was'. Fiona was beautiful in every way and she certainly made a very beautiful bride. Most females even those who are not normally known for their beauty seem to excel themselves on their wedding day. Fiona was no exception shining like a beacon of beauty and light.

Everything went well. A perfect Easter wedding, it could be said, yet not an expensive one. The ceremony was held at All Saints Parish Church situated in the High Street, Northallerton. This beautiful church stood on a site where people have worshipped since the 7th Century.

Neil visualised Fiona coming down the aisle, 'or perhaps I should call it the nave' he recalled. It had been explained to him that the correct name for what he called the middle aisle in the church was the nave. She walked slowly and elegantly accompanied by her father, with Jenny her resplendent Matron of Honour following, to the sound of the majestic church organ. He remembers as he stood with Dave his best man, facing what was called the 'crossing' where the vows were to be said. He thought, 'I just could not resist a fleeting glance over my shoulder to see her' as he stood at the front. Even the veil was unable to disguise her beauty as it shone through the lace.

Whilst this was one of the happiest of days, it was tense to start with. It meant a lot to both of them and to the members of the family that were in attendance. Fiona and Jenny had hit it off really well and were almost like sisters and were now to become sisters-in-law. Being already married Jenny was Fiona's Matron of Honour. Although it was slightly unusual for someone from the groom's side to take such a position, Fiona insisted that was what would make her happy, and so that is how it was.

Neil was aware that everyone was praying, especially him, that the ceremony and reception would go without a hitch. Even those who were not closely involved wished nothing but the best for the husband and wife to be. Until the ceremony is over and a few drinks have been downed it is natural for there to be a mixture of excitement, expectation and nervousness making the atmosphere in the church at least a little tense.

The tension was getting to Neil for as he tried to place the ring on Fiona's finger his hands shook. In fact, most of his body was shaking. Horror! He had dropped the ring! 'Shit!' he said to himself, as he dived to the floor to start looking and immediately felt very guilty for cursing in church even though it was under his breath and no one but he and the good Lord heard it. He was quickly joined by Dave and it was a sight to behold the both of them on all fours frantically doing a fingertip search of the area.

"Darling, what are you doing?" Fiona asked.

"Trying to find your ring," he answered and looked up at her questioningly, thinking 'It's pretty obvious what I am doing' and went back to his frantic searching. Churches are not known for their brightness, and certainly, the light was sparse at ground level.

"Stop, stop," she insisted.

They both stood up and she bent down. Putting her fingers into the turn-up of Neil's left trouser leg she pulled out the ring.

"I just happened to see where it fell," she commented sweetly as they gazed at her wondering how on earth she had done that.

The whole church seemed to heave a sigh of relief, the guests laughed and gave a spontaneous round of applause then settled down to enjoy the rest of the service. Even the vicar had a very broad smile on what normally seemed a very long face. Neil was now feeling much more relaxed. The incident had broken the ice and released the tension for him and the whole congregation.

[Briefly, back at the flat]

Neil started to chuckle as he turned another page and seeing photographs of the reception recalled Dave his best man giving his speech.

[At the reception; we join about halfway through Dave's speech as best man.]

"....*but the customer said,* **It wasn't the new coat of paint that killed my budgie, it was the blow lamp!***"*

The audience roared with laughter once more at yet another funny punch line. Dave looked up from his notes and said...

"I know we are all laughing now, and I thank you for that, but have you noticed there is also an awful lot of crying goes on at weddings." Dave pointed to the pyramid-like structure near to him. It was covered in white icing, balanced on columns and in the middle of the table. He joked, *"Can you see? Even the cake is in tiers!"*

As this wasn't his best joke there was more of a groan to this one. But hey, the audience were all behind him and very happy for Fiona and Neil. It showed on their faces and by the way they were enjoying themselves. Dave was off again...

"I was talking to Neil and a few of the lads just moments ago over a pint and we were kidding him on about getting married, you know, as lads do. Another good man bites the dust and all those sorts of jibes. I said to him are you going to be a **man** *and take Fiona tonight or are you going to be a* **mouse** *and put it off till tomorrow night. He said I'm a* **rat** *I took her last night."*

This one really caught them off guard and most fell about laughing apart from the aged Aunt Marissa in the corner who, by her face, had either never had the pleasure or had no idea what the inference was. Someone was still trying to explain the joke to her when Dave began again.

"We all know that Neil and Fiona are Christians so I took the opportunity to get them something religious as a wedding present. I bought them each a little framed religious text to inspire them. They are intended to hang on the wall above their bed. The one I got for Fiona reads, **I need thee every hour** *and the one for Neil's side of the bed read,* **Lord, give me strength.***"*

Real hearty belly laughs could be heard to this. One guest even fell off his chair, whilst another choked on her drink; they found it so funny and unexpected. The laughter lasted a lot longer this time 'I think I left the best one till last' he thought, feeling very satisfied at his performance. The noise and laughter finally petered out. 'But I am enjoying this, so just one more' Dave thought.

"I am sure that Fiona can't wait to **sink** *into Neil's* **arms**. *What she hasn't thought about is spending the rest of her life with her* **arms** *in his* **sink."**

Again, this caused lots of frivolity but at that point Dave got down to the business of thanking people, reading out a few of the cards and proposing the toasts, receiving a huge round of applause at the end. During the card reading, he said, *"Now this one is a special card"* paused for effect and then continued *"It is from me....... It reads "If an apple a day keeps the doctor away, what will a pair do at night?"* He just could not resist getting another laugh in before he had finished.

The dancing was led by Neil and Fiona doing the smooch and after a couple of laps, or perhaps I should say a few sways, everyone else started to join in and those who could dance properly did something a bit more energetic and somewhat more technical.

Finally, Neil and Fiona jumped into the taxi and left the reception for their honeymoon. Shouts of good wishes were ringing in their ears and the enthusiastic crowd gave them another covering of confetti from head to foot with even more having fallen all around them. A brief stop at home to get changed and try to rid themselves of confetti which still appeared, in the most unlikely of places, from time to time weeks later. Picking up their luggage they were off to sunny Spain.

[Thoughts return to the present]

'How happy we were on our special day,' Neil thought as he closed the album and looked down at his feet. He chuckled to himself, 'You know I have another pair of shoes just like this in the cupboard. Now I really must get ready, I want to get there and back before it gets too late in the day.'

Replacing his slipper on his left foot for a shoe, so both feet matched, he then shook off the water from the flowers and rewrapped them. He picked up one or two cleaning implements, to help him tidy up the grave and headstone, put them into the boot of his car and set off on his journey to the cemetery in Northallerton.

He now had a Ford Cortina. He was going to replace his wrecked Morris Minor with another similar model but decided against it. Instead, he went for something completely different and just a little bit sporty.

Neil's journey to the cemetery was quite uneventful and as he often did he filled his mind with times gone by spent with Fiona. This time he thought about their last Christmas preparations.

[A few days before Christmas 1960]

Christmas was a very special time of year for Neil.

"He's a big kid at heart," Fiona used to tell people proudly. Perhaps, instead, he was just not the sort of adult that tried to hide his feelings. He decided 'It is sad that some adults, mainly men, pretend not to be interested in Christmas. Perhaps they think it makes them more macho. Either that or it is so they get out of doing any of the card writing, present buying, present wrapping, decoration hanging, Christmas-Tree dressing, or Christmas dinner cooking. But they still enjoy the fruit of all the wife's efforts that make the season special.'

Neil loved it, got involved in just about every aspect and was quite happy everyone knew he loved it. He was so pleased that Fiona also enjoyed the season. They hung coloured paper decorations from the ceiling, corner to corner. Hung balloons in each corner of the room. They decorated the tree with bright shiny baubles and tinsel then lit it up with coloured lights.

"Santa's Grotto," judged Fiona as she stood back and admired their handy work and the huge, green, luscious, 6ft 6inch **real** Christmas

tree. This was now reaching over 7ft, having been loaded into a sturdy pot, and was nearly touching the ceiling.

"It really looks great," agreed Neil standing close behind her holding the mistletoe above their heads, *"and can you smell the pine?"*

Realising he must be standing very close behind her; Fiona turned and in doing so, landed in his arms. Well, into his one arm, his other one was employed holding up the mistletoe. She immediately realised what Neil was up to. They did not need mistletoe for a kiss - but kissed they did. The mistletoe soon discarded 'I want both arms for this' he decided.

"That's one of the many things I love about you," Fiona whispered. *"You are so romantic,"* and kissed Neil again. The magic was always there between them but this time one thing could not be allowed to lead to another because there was work to be done. Dragging herself reluctantly from Neil's embrace Fiona said *"But sorry not today,"* she added with a genuine apologetic look on her face. *"There is far too much to do."*

Reluctantly Neil let her go. *"You're right and by the time we have finished we will both deserve an early night,"* he said winking. Then as she walked away he quickly swung his hand and planted a loving smack on her bottom.

It was just a few days before Christmas and they had already done a lot of their preparations. They had delayed putting the tree up till that day because it was a real tree and they wanted it to last.

"I am still finding pine needles from last year," said Fiona as she started to tidy away the boxes and leftover decorations. Then added *"Pine needles and confetti,"* and they both laughed out loud.

She sat on the floor and looked up at the tree. Then in a sort of longing yearning manner, she said: *"One year we will be wrapping toys and other presents and putting them under the tree for our son or daughter."* She longed to become a mother but realised that it was best to plan a family properly. They were very rich in many ways but not very well off financially and had both agreed to wait for a while and save up. Having a child would mean Fiona leaving work. No-way would she want someone else to bring her children up, especially in their formative years and anyway paying someone else to do her job as a mother would mean it was a waste of time her working to earn money.

Fiona had a pretty good job as a secretary for a large department store and Neil was now a fully qualified mechanic for Smurthwaites. They had both agreed to save and were doing very well but he knew it was difficult for Fiona. He too wanted to have children but was a little more pragmatic than Fiona. This wasn't something that they argued about, quite the contrary they were both in full agreement and that is why it was working. They decided it would be at least another year before they would start a family.

If they knew what tragedy was to befall them it may have made their thinking and actions completely different. Of course, they did not know this was to be their last Christmas together.

Neil spoke, *"We have a lot to look forward to darling,"* and tried to cheer a slightly sad-faced Fiona, having to be patient for motherhood.

"Yes, you're right!" Fiona sprung, both, up off the floor and out of her momentary melancholy. *"Talking of looking forward, how about inviting Jenny and her family for Christmas Day?"* Both Fiona and Neil were very close to Jenny and got on very well with Bill. They often met up with their whole family which included the children, Ken and Beth. *"There will be six of us all together and I will enjoy cooking for lots of people,"* she continued jokingly, *"It will give me some practice ready for when we too have a big family to feed."*

"How many children are you planning on having?" asked Neil, who was taken aback a bit but catching on to the joke.

"Well, I hope to have at least another fifteen years before my childbearing days will be over. You work it out at one per year," Fiona suggested trying to look serious.

"We will have to replace this house with a castle!" Neil jested.

"Ha ha - That would be wonderful," were Fiona's parting words as she took the rubbish outside to throw into the bin.

[Approaching the cemetery on the 2nd Anniversary of Fiona's death]

With happy Jingle bells still ringing in his ears, but sad thoughts of things that were never to be, Neil drove down the High Street, the road leading to the cemetery.

As he parked up, his mind was back firmly in the present. He retrieved the cleaning utensils and roses from the boot and walked in the direction of the cemetery gates. He looked with a fondness for a few moments at the parish church where he was married to Fiona and used to attend most Sundays for communion. He also thought sadly about not having been able to attend her funeral held in the same church.

Turning back towards the cemetery he could see the familiar sight of the Lodge House at the entrance a short distance away. He walked through the huge metal gates and made his way to where Fiona was laid to rest. As he approached he thought 'the grave looks good' if that's the right phrase to use for a grave. He was not at all surprised to see lots of other flowers at the graveside.

There were some lovely bouquets there but his attention was immediately drawn to a bunch of quite bright yet beautiful flowers that seemed to stand out. He read the card, which simply said, 'So sorry!' and was unsigned. The quality of the flowers was outstanding, it was in its own vase specially designed to be pushed into the earth and it was plain to see that no expense had been spared.

'Who could they be from?' He wondered as he checked both sides of the card. 'No signature.' Everyone was sorry that Fiona had died so he thought nothing unusual about the sentiment expressed on the card.

Neil fully expected to shed a tear that day at some point but he did not expect it to happen so soon. Among the bouquets, there was naturally one from Jenny. When he read Jenny's words on the card he could not help himself. She had written 'From Jenny with all my love to the sister I miss so much.'

He tidied up the grave, washed the stone and readjusted all the flowers as well as adding his roses.

He stayed and talked to Fiona for quite some time, just as if she was standing beside him. He did not know what heaven was like but just had to have faith for his own sanity that, wherever it was and whatever it was like, it was a good place where Fiona could be happy and safe. The picture that came to his mind that was most comforting was the image he had of Jesus Christ cradling her in His outstretched arms. He had to believe that Fiona, this most precious of God's creations was now being cherished in the hands of her maker.

Just before he departed, he blew a kiss towards the grave. In his mind, of course, he was blowing it to Fiona herself.

"God bless you my darling," he said out loud and walked slowly and tearfully back to the car. He did not stick around any longer having been there the best part of thirty minutes. 'I bet she is watching over me,' he thought trying to reassure himself and bring a little cheer to his time of sadness. Starting to feel more and more depressed he turned on the car radio and sang to the pop tunes as he drove back to Scarborough.

Neil was a very tender-hearted man but wasn't soft and would not allow people to walk all over him. He certainly stood up for his rights when the need arose but, unlike a lot of men, he was easily brought to tears because he cared so much about others. When he visited the cemetery he often had a walk around and read the messages on other gravestones. Some of them were very sad indeed. Graves of children, who had died at an early age, for example, moved him.

Gradually, as he journeyed home, his demeanour lightened and he was cheered by the music. His thoughts turned more to the future. He was going to have to get a job soon or he would have to start selling things like his car. 'Dread the thought' he mused 'It would be very difficult then to visit Fiona or for that matter my Jenny' who still lived in Northallerton.

CHAPTER FIVE: Just Good Friends.

[Back at Spinetti's Cafe September 1963]

Neil and Helen were still engrossed in what each other had to say whilst many other customers had come and gone. As time did not seem to matter they sipped the last drop from their second cup. Luigi began to rub his hands as Helen came to order yet more frothy coffee. She insisted that Neil let her pay for these.

Meanwhile, Neil allowed his mind to wander and he pondered about Luigi who was seemingly a bit of an enigma. Whilst he showed obvious delight in the money coming in – the more the merrier, he was not at all a miser or a Scrooge. He often helped worthy local causes and probably (although Neil did not know for sure) gave money to charity. He had had a very tough life when he first landed in England as a refugee. He arrived with his wife and six children and just a few liras in his pocket after he had lost everything in Italy. The Germans who were for a while on the same side as the Italians, under the madman Mussolini, were quick to take retribution when their alliance broke down. The Spinetti family were lucky to escape with their lives.

It is no wonder then, that he should show delight hearing the till ring, knowing how difficult it had been to even survive and what a struggle it was for him to get a business started. He never again wanted to revisit those times of old.

Helen arrived with the coffee and they began again their conversation. The more they talked the more Neil opened out to her about what had happened to him, how much he loved Fiona and all that he knew about the crash and his battle to get back to full health. This it seemed made Helen look very uncomfortable. She went very pale produced more tears and a lot of agitated fidgeting. 'She seems a very nice and obviously a very sensitive person,' decided Neil 'She showed great sympathy and seemed to agonise for me when I explained what I had gone through.'

Once the subject was changed she became calm and the atmosphere brightened up. Neil was conscious that Helen was moving her chair, every so often, just a little closer to his. They were both now very relaxed and Helen became a little flirtatious. Her body language said 'I want to be more than just friends.'

It was now nearing the end of their marathon chat and sponsored coffee drinking session, which was so epic it should really have been done to raise money for charity.

Choosing his words very carefully Neil brought their meeting to a close by saying, *"Look I do not wish to be presumptive Helen, but I must tell you I am not looking for love. No one can ever replace Fiona and I want you to be aware of that because I would not want to mislead you."*

Helen squeezed Neil's arm and said softly, *"I understand."*

"However, you said you liked me." Helen nodded as if to confirm her feelings. Neil continued, *"And I do like you."* He paused then admitted, *"It can sometimes be very lonely...,"* then paused again as if, for a short while he was in another world, then said. *"Look, what I am trying to say is....can we be friends?"*

She seemed delighted, *"Yes of course,"* and with that, they arranged to meet again for coffee at the end of the week and went their separate ways.

Neil was very drawn to Helen. The same unexplained feeling he had when they first met on the beach stayed with him and if anything grew stronger. He knew she was very attracted to him for it was plain for everyone to see. Yet he just could not let this happen. He fought it every inch of the way and even made up reasons for not seeing her for a while. It was very difficult for him because whilst he did not want to lose her, Neil also felt that he should not allow their relationship to become anything more than one of friendship. This meant that he had to sometimes appear a little colder towards her than perhaps other friends would be.

He put two rules in place that he strictly kept to. These were to make sure they did not meet in the evening or be anywhere alone together. Whilst Helen was not directly aware of these rules she was certainly aware of his reluctance to meet under those circumstances. She had agreed to just be friends and after a while got into the habit but she always wished for more. Without making herself appear cheap or in any way easy, she did use a lot of her feminine charm in an attempt to take the relationship further. This made life even more difficult for Neil so he would engineer long gaps between their outings to allow himself to regroup. These gaps would be punctuated by the occasional telephone conversation. All this was difficult for both of them but their friendship blossomed. Finances got a little easier for Neil when he was offered a part-time job at a local car repair shop in January of 1964. It also gave him another excuse to see a little less of Helen.

The rule about not meeting in the evening was relaxed providing Neil knew that there would be plenty of other people around. After restricting themselves to having lunch together they started from time to time meeting up for an evening meal in a local restaurant or a drink or two at a local pub. They had many outings in the months that followed, cinema, theatre etc. They had lots of fun and really enjoyed each other's company.

[York March 1964]

One of their most memorable day trips was to York. They both loved York from previous visits, they had made separately, Helen with her husband and Neil with Fiona. They agreed that the ancient history of the City and its magnificent buildings and architecture were a sight to behold. The quaint streets, alleyways and, what are called, snickelways hold a lot of history and mystery and are truly intriguing.

"If buildings could talk I bet they would have some interesting stories to tell," commented Helen, as they walked down one of York's most famous streets.

"Yes but, I don't think much of this part of York, do you?" claimed Neil in a very serious voice.

"*Really, why is that?*" questioned Helen finding his remark very strange, considering he had done nothing but heap praise on all that this wonderful city had to offer.

"*It's a shambles!*" Neil delivered the punch line. They both laughed, not a lot, because it wasn't one of his best jokes but it was still funny.

As they walked down the street arm-in-arm they chatted, joked and laughed. What a good day out they were having. The arm-in-arm link just felt comfortable they were just good friends and that is not an innuendo, I really do mean, they were just good friends. They had got a lot closer as friends as time went by but this was still a platonic relationship and not more than the odd kiss on the cheek and a few hugs had passed between them over the last few months. They chatted about the types of buildings, especially those in the Shambles as they now walked along Parliament Street.

Neil always insisted that Helen, or any other female he accompanied along the pavement, should walk on the inside while he walked near the kerb.

"*Why is that?*" inquired Helen.

"*I believe it dates back to the time when there were a lot of streets like the Shambles where the upstairs part of each house hung out over the pavement. No underground sewers or dustbin men in those days. Any rubbish or unmentionable waste that the householder wanted rid of was jettisoned out of the top window straight down on to the street below. So keeping the lady protected was the chivalrous and well-mannered thing to do. I still keep up the tradition because even on a modern road it means the lady is furthest from the danger of vehicles and any dust kicked or water sprayed up.*"

"Well, how sweet," Helen praised Neil, "and how romantic. I am very impressed."

Crossing the road at the opening to St Sampson's Square they were just about to enter Davygate when…

"Mary, is that you Mary?" came a shout from a long way off and again, **"Mary, wait…"** This time the woman doing the shouting was waving her arm, seemingly in their direction. Helen immediately dropped her head and steered them into the nearest shop.

"Let's go in here," she asked, question-like, but her body language wasn't giving Neil a choice as she steered them both off the street and through the doors of Browns Department Store.

The subject they were talking about and the direction in which they were moving had suddenly changed. Neil thought 'Funny!' and said, *"That woman, the one who was shouting, seemed to throw you off course a bit. It was almost as if she was trying to attract your attention or that of someone near to us."*

"No not me," assured Helen. *"If she was then she must have got me mixed up with someone else. Look at that lovely dress. I wonder how much it is?"* dismissing Neil's perception of the situation and quickly changing the subject. *"That's quite reasonable,"* she said as she read the ticket, and then moved on to the next display.

After spending a good twenty minutes, dragging Neil with her and getting them lost in the crowds; doing a lot of looking at clothes, a lot of looking around her and over her shoulder, Helen, much to Neil's disgust, had not bought anything. She suggested enthusiastically *"I know let's go and have a look around the Minster."*

"But you haven't bought anything. All these very lovely dresses, bags and shoes and you haven't found anything you like?" he questioned.

"Yes, I have seen lots of things I would like to buy, but if we are going to do some more sightseeing we do not want to have to carry stuff around do we?" replied Helen. *"We can always come back this way."*

"*Yes OK!*" Neil agreed realising it would probably be him that had to do the carrying. He liked antiques, history and old buildings, particularly churches and cathedrals. So he quite liked Helen's idea to visit the Minster and went on to say, "*So York Minster here we come. Did you know there's no better place than the top of York Minster's medieval central tower to get a bird's eye view of the city? They reckon at 230 feet it's the highest point in the whole of York.*"

"*You seem to know a lot about it,*" she remarked. "*Of course - you have been before. I didn't go to the Minster and was not really all that aware of the tower when I last visited York, it will be a new experience for me.*"

They wound their way towards York Minster via the snickelways including Stonegate and Minstergate.
"*Mind you, it's a very long and winding journey to the top of the tower. You will need to climb 275 steps. Are you up to it?*" asked Neil.
"*You could always carry me,*" joked Helen. At least Neil was hoping she was joking. Arriving at the Minster she said, "*It is very impressive isn't it?*"
"*It certainly is,*" answered Neil. "*They say it's the largest gothic cathedral in Northern Europe.*"

The huge windows and magnificent architecture seemed to take their breath away. They marvelled at the stained glass masterpieces and beautifully carved stonework before venturing up the steps of the tower.

Helen, a little unsure about her level of fitness, suggested, "*I think we ought to attempt the tower steps now before we tire ourselves out too much walking around.*"

"*Yes you're probably right,*" agreed Neil and they made their way towards the tower entrance. "*We can always pick up where we left off,*" he added.

"*Yes, if we have any energy left,*" chirped in Helen, losing confidence at the thought of all those steps.

They set off up the steps, taking it very slowly. *"We need to pace ourselves,"* advised Neil.

"Good idea," said Helen, as she patted Neil on the back.

They managed the steps - just. Even for a couple of youngsters who were fairly fit it was a long, steep, testing journey. They paused every so often to get their breath and take in the spectacle of the medieval pinnacles and gothic gargoyles. Stepping out into the open air was their reward, the best panoramic views of York's picturesque city centre. They could see the hidden alleyways and medieval lanes that they had travelled, and beyond the city, the beautiful surroundings of the Yorkshire countryside. They stood close together taking in the view and breathing heavily from the exertion of their climbing efforts.

Having got her breath back, *"This has been such a wonderful day,"* said Helen, turning, coming even closer to Neil and staring directly into his eyes. Helen's close approach gave him no option but to return the stare. She asked, *"Isn't the scenery beautiful?"* Meaning the countryside of course but said it in a very soft and seductive tone.
Neil was slightly taken aback by the closeness of their faces. He realised, not for the first time, just what a beautiful sight he saw before him, especially her big brown eyes. He answered, emphatically, echoing her tone, while captured trance-like in that moment, *"Yes, very beautiful."*

This was a wonderful setting; the most romantic 'kissing scene' that any Hollywood movie director would be proud of. The atmosphere, the view, the venue and the scent of love on the breeze heightened the unseen magnetism drawing their lips closer and closer.

"Chrue! Chrue!" Neil turned away coughing, took out his handkerchief, and continued to deal with this sudden coughing fit that was gripping him. 'Phew, that was close' he thought immediately regretting what he had done. Not the near kiss it was the phoney cough he regretted.

Helen secretly thought 'I will get you one day Mr Collins' enjoying their friendship but so wishing they could be more than just good friends.

Despite the incident in the tower or perhaps because of it they did have a very good day and thoroughly enjoyed it.

This had been just one of the many outings that Helen and Neil shared. As time went by it was getting more and more difficult for Neil to keep Helen at arm's length so to speak. Helen was trying her best, without making it too obvious, being careful not to break his trust, to woo Neil with the hope he would fall in love with her. She knew how she felt and that she wanted much more from their relationship.

Neil was being very strong but sometimes felt as though he was at times weakening. He questioned himself, even argued with himself about his feelings towards Helen. He was sure she wanted them to be lovers and he did not want to push her away because he valued their friendship but he just did not dare, if that is the right word, to allow himself the freedom to give in to her female charms and attraction. 'Do I love her?' he would ask himself. He could not or did not answer. Perhaps he was afraid of the truth. So difficult, though it was for both, they continued to be - just good friends.

CHAPTER SIX:
Close Encounter of the Intimate Kind.

[In the newsagent's shop, 3rd May 1964]

"Well - I am really glad for you," said John as he served Neil with his usual newspaper. *"I have noticed a lady with you, from time to time and you certainly seem a lot chirpier these days."*

"Well early days yet," replied Neil not wanting to go into too much detail but enjoying the fact that he did feel a lot better since Helen came into his life.

"What are your plans for today Neil?"

"I need to concentrate a bit more on getting a job," Neil said thinking about having to write more letters.

"I thought you had a job at a garage?" John questioned.

"Yes but that is only part-time. It is better than nothing until I get a proper full-time position. Better have another one of those writing pads please John," then turned to look at the greetings cards. It was Helen's birthday. He spent quite some time trying to find the ideal card. Not wanting to give the wrong impression it should not be too friendly, or soppy, but one that would let her know she was very much appreciated.

As it was Helen's birthday he had invited her around to his flat that evening for a meal. She had visited before during the day and shared a cuppa but never in the evening. He was fully aware that this would break the rules he had set out for their relationship which were in place to prevent, to put it bluntly, any likelihood of, what his Aunty Annie would have called - hanky-panky.

Was Neil now saying it was time? No, he was very confused and not at all sure that inviting her was the correct thing to do. At that time all he was sure of was, 'it is her birthday, a special occasion, which calls for something special for a special friend.'

Back at the flat, as he cleaned and vacuumed, he continued to wonder whether or not he was doing the right thing. Was this liable to make her think there may be more on offer than just a platonic friendship? In fact was he now in the right place, mentally, to be able to get closer to someone else. If he did allow the relationship to change how would he feel? Would he feel guilty as if it was unfaithful to Fiona, or would he go along with the belief that Fiona would want him to live a full life and find someone new?

Neil knew that most men, and he was no exception, needed the intimate sexual closeness of a woman. Some sleep around to try and achieve that but very rarely does promiscuity truly satisfy that need. 'Those needs' he decided 'could only be properly addressed and substantially fulfilled when the couple are in love.' He was not of the promiscuous ilk and had remained celibate for a long time now. Though he had to admit that being close to Helen had started to bring on urges. Physical things his body needed and fanciful ideas of the mind. What he did not know was if it would be the right thing. His morals, linked to his loyalty to the memory of Fiona, had so far helped to control his natural instincts.

After writing and posting more job applications he spent the rest of the day cooking and cleaning in preparation for Helen's birthday celebration.

Finally, he showered away the day's stress and sweat. Sweat for obvious reasons he had worked hard and was not at all used to cooking. Well only for himself and certainly not a three-course candlelit meal. Nearly all the meals in years gone by had been cooked first by Auntie Annie followed by Fiona. If he had not from time to time helped Fiona and learned from her in the kitchen he would probably now have been living on tinned stuff.

That's another worry, 'better leave out the candles' he thought. Right up to the last minute he argued with himself as to whether candles were a good idea. Stress was from the increasing need to find a job but also he wanted tonight to be special, very special. Most of all stress because he was still arguing with himself as to whether he should allow his natural desires towards Helen to have their way or fight it with all his strength. 'Candles or no candles?' he went over and over 'Candles or no candles?' This was a difficult one. 'I know' he confidently decided, 'I will place the candle holders on the table and have the candles near at hand. If things are going....' He paused a moment, candlesticks in hand, '....well shall we say in the direction that they may, I can add the candles later without even attempting to light them. Unless of course the ambience warms up and becomes candle-like........a bit wicked.'

Even with those slightly naughty thoughts going through his mind he was still confused as to how to deal with his feelings. After drying himself on a large blue towel he splashed himself with a little bit more Old Spice than normal just in case! He knew Helen liked the aroma because she had commented previously on how nice he smelt.

Helen always smelled good. She told Neil the perfume she wore was called 'In love'. He was going to buy her that for her birthday but thought it a bit too intimate as a present for someone who was just a friend. When I say just a friend I don't mean it how it sounds – she was not *just* a friend, as if being just a friend was something less valued. On the contrary, he valued her worth and their friendship, very highly.

Seven o'clock on-the-dot there came a knocking at the door. He welcomed her with a more enthusiastic hug than ever before. In the past, hugs were not that frequent and when they happened they were never like that one.

"Happy birthday Helen," Neil announced.

"Thank you. I have been looking forward to this evening," beamed Helen.

"Me too," agreed Neil taking her coat and hanging it up in the cupboard.

Helen took up her usual seat on the chair just across from the couch where Neil usually sits.

"What would you like to drink?" He asked as he grabbed the bottle of vodka.

"I'll have a Vodka and orange please."

'Thought so' he said to himself as he then started to pour it. After a drink or two he, well actually both of them, became more relaxed.

"I have a present for you," Neil said out of the blue.

"Oh! Wonderful! How nice of you Neil." Helen's face, already glowing from the alcohol, lit up even more.

"But you will have to come over here and sit beside me to receive it," said Neil cheekily, as he patted the space on the couch beside him.

Helen's mind worked over time. 'Was this to be a gift in kind?' Her heart began to beat a little faster as she took the two or three steps and sat down beside Neil. She felt very excited that perhaps; just perhaps, this might be the moment she had been waiting for, even subconsciously, praying for.

Neil grabbed a nicely wrapped, large, square, very thin parcel from behind the couch and presented it to her.

"Oh! Thank you. I just love getting presents," remarked Helen thinking how silly she had been to get all excited but did not show her disappointment outwardly. *"I wonder what it could be?"* she said knowingly, as it was obvious to anyone that it was an L.P.[8], even before it was unwrapped. She tore carefully at the paper to reveal her favourite group's new long-playing record; The Beatles Second Album.

"Wow!" she exclaimed, *"Thank you so much,"* as she tore off the last of the pretty pink paper. Helen added, *"That's really great!"* as she laid it

down on the coffee table, threw her arms around Neil and gave him a big smacker of a kiss on the cheek.

This time, after the kiss, he did not let her go but pulled her very slowly back towards him with the full intention of kissing her square on the lips and making it quite clear how he felt. Was this a subconscious decision, an impulse or something secretly planned in advance? Perhaps it was planned but either he did not really know or just did not want to admit it. What he did know was that a decision, after much soul searching, had finally been reached.

Surprised at first she soon realised that this really was the moment she had been waiting for and kissed him in return with a passion. They parted lips, momentarily, as if to take a breath and resumed the contact. Lips opened and tongues said everything without a word being spoken. This would certainly be a night to remember.

As things started to really heat up between them, Helen whispered, *"Let's put the lights out. It's so much more romantic, don't you think?"*

Neil, if a little unsure did not answer verbally, thinking it a rhetorical question. He accepted her reasoning and answered by carrying out her request. After all, he wasn't going to do anything to spoil the moment. Having dutifully switched off the lights he stumbled, a little in the dark, as he returned to her side and fell once more on to her partially clothed body.

From that moment words were unspoken and apart from the clock chiming from time to time and their occasional murmurs and gasps of delight, there was little or no noise apart from the distant noise of the traffic from the road outside.

Whilst the ears had a rest, along with the eyes, in the now darkened room the other senses were certainly being employed. Nostrils delighted at the aroma of perfumes. The names of both 'love and spice' seemed to have been an omen, a forecast, of what that evening was to bring. The sense of touch through hands and skin contact giving that unique tantalising feeling that only occurs when two human bodies are in close rapture. Not to mention the indescribable touch/taste sensation for the giver and receiver when lips and tongue perform to create a rainbow of magical experiences when seeking and finding intimate places.

Clothes were left where they fell. So urgent was the need to stay in each other's grasp and make the most of the moment. They made no attempt to go to the bedroom. All that pent up desire and dormant passion were set free.

After a period of calm following the gentle, tender, yet passionate storm, Helen said, with a great deal of gratification in her voice. *"Well, I have waited an awfully long time for that. Once you make up your mind you certainly know how to sweep a girl off her feet."*

"Thank you for being a girl very worthy of being swept off her feet. In fact, as I recall you were doing quite a lot of the sweeping yourself," Neil answered continuing the metaphor.

They both laughed and hugged. Neil suddenly jumped up. **"Oh, hell!"** he cursed and ran to the kitchen, still naked. Well, the meal was not burned but other things nearly were as he got too close to the stove. Luckily it had been warming very, very, slowly, the meal that is, on the lowest of gases.

Whilst Neil was staving off disaster in the kitchen, for the meal and his manhood, Helen quickly got dressed and switched on the light. Neil followed suit soon after.

Needless to say, Neil lit the candles. The meal was a little on the dry side but as they were washing it down with a bottle of very wet wine it was just fine. Helen did say she enjoyed the meal and Neil just hoped she wasn't saying that just to be kind.
Feeling everything was good in the world they made themselves comfortable on the couch and listened to Helen's new record, playing softly in the background.

"This has been the best and most memorable birthday I have ever had," confirmed Helen.

"Yes," agreed Neil. "I shall certainly remember it as well." He looked directly into her eyes and said so very sincerely "It has been sensational, you were sensational. Thank you so very much indeed," and with that, kissed her again.

They stayed very close together on the couch chatting, holding hands, laughing, kissing occasionally and whispering sweet nothings.

The night was now nearly over when Helen asked, "You know how you are finding it difficult to get a full-time job?"

"Yes, no luck so far," Neil agreed.

"Well, as you know, my dad owns a factory and is now, at last, in a position to think about expanding. I am sure he would be willing to find a position for you. It may only be labouring or something menial to start with but I am sure you would go on to prove your worth and earn promotion." Without waiting for a reply, "That's his number," she said pushing a business card into his hand.

Neil read it. It said 'Crosby's Aluminium Foundry, Queen Margaret's Industrial Estate, Queen Margaret's Road, Scarborough.' It had the owners name Ronald Crosby and a telephone number.

"I will see him in the morning. Shall I tell him to expect your call?" added Helen encouragingly.

"Aluminium eh? Emm.... what sort of things does he make?" Neil asked not knowing if it would be right for him, but still willing to give it a try.

"Just anything small that can be made lighter or cheaper or both, out of aluminium" she replied. "Like sculptures, memorial plaques, house or business nameplates or other signs."

Neil stood up and put the card on the table. "OK, I will give it a go. Thank you." Changing the subject he turned and stared down into Helen's captivating eyes. Neil knew that he was now besotted and looked upon that evening as being a turning point in his life. *"Darling,"* he said and was just about to add something when Helen stood up...

"That is the first time," Helen interrupted.

Not really following what she meant he repeated what Helen had just said as a question *"That's the first time?"*

"You called me darling for the first time," answered Helen excitedly. *"Please say it again."*

"Darling," Neil said, this time even more sincerely and soulfully, and again *"darling,"* as he reached out to take her in his arms and added, *"Tonight has been a very big night for firsts."*

"You have no idea what hearing that means to me. I love you; I love you so much it hurts. I have loved you since the moment we first met on the sands." Her tears of joy were plain to see and they started to trickle down her cheeks and transferred to Neil's face as she pulled him close.

Neil fought to control his own emotions as he squeezed her tight as if to assure her he would never let her go.

Once again calm returned and emotions subsided. They sat down and Neil then continued as he had first intended. *"Darling, I really do mean it when I say tonight has been so wonderful, you are so wonderful, and I am sorry for being such a fool and not being sure before today that we were right for each other."*

"Yes, tonight has been so wonderful," Helen echoed and trying to lighten the mood a little. *"Even the meal turned out to be very tasty considering the chef was busy elsewhere seeing to his customer's other needs."* They both chuckled.

"We must do it again soon," Neil enthused and quickly confirmed. *"The whole evening I mean."*

"Of course, I know **exactly** *what you mean,* **darling,**" putting on a posh voice and playfully pushing a gentle finger into his arm, adding to the embarrassment he must have felt. Helen knew he was not just referring to their lovemaking, but certainly hoped they were going to repeat that many times as well. *"Why not let me return the compliment. Come to my house for dinner next time,"* Helen suggested.

"That sounds good," Neil agreed and they made plans for the following week as well as a date to meet at Spinetti's the day after tomorrow. Hearing the sound of a car pulling up outside he said, *"Actually that sounds like your taxi."*

"Goodness is that the time," Helen disbelievingly looked at her watch. It was quite a big watch with a very wide strap. 'Rather strange for a ladies watch to be so big,' thought Neil. 'Cumbersome one might even say. It looks very expensive she must be quite attached to it because she didn't take it off all night.'

He was aware that she appeared to be reasonably financially well off. He did not know for sure but got that impression. Why she didn't own a car he did not know.
Not for driving tonight, while drinking, but he noticed she never drove anywhere and always walked or travelled by bus and sometimes a taxi. In fact, there were quite a few things that Neil did not know about Helen but he pushed all that to the back of his mind.

Now, any slight sense of being unsure about her had vanished. The night they had just enjoyed and thoughts of the many wonderful hours that he would spend with her in the future filled his mind with good thoughts.

Helen gathered her belongings especially her birthday card and new record. Her hands were full but her lips were very available. The goodnight kiss on the doorstep was interrupted by the impatient taxi driver blowing his horn.

"Thank you for <u>everything!</u>" she shouted as she boarded the taxi and sent a kiss winging its way through the air to Neil before shutting the car door. She waved through the back window all the way down the street.

"Yesss!" Neil said out loud and gently punched the air with both hands after shutting the front door of his flat. Very happy with how the evening turned out. This outward expression of joy was tempered with an inner prayer that it met with Fiona's approval and a thank you to God for his goodness.

The relationship flourished. Helen and Neil experienced many happy days together at home and away. Neil was taken on by Helen's father Ronald Crosby known as Ron to his friends but as Mr Crosby to most of the foundry workers and to Neil at first. Neil soon became an important key worker in the foundry.

Helen's divorce did eventually come through and they, well Neil, often broached the subject of getting married yet when they did discuss it he felt she was holding back. 'Perhaps she is just not ready or having gone through a divorce doesn't want to go down that road again' Neil thought understandingly.

[Whilst the sixties, was a very exciting time with, the music, contraception, drugs, fashion, sex and other things that made people feel there were new freedoms, it was still the norm to get married, and preferably before having babies.]

Up till 1961 when the contraceptive pill came on to the market Neil and Fiona had to either use the withdrawal method or a condom, and he wasn't keen on either. The only other form of contraception, widely available, was abstinence and that was definitely out of the question.

Neil was certainly not into drugs and as has already been mentioned did not sleep around. Even though the world was changing, and to a great degree the moral decline of the country had started to set in, marriage at that time, was still considered to be an important part of social etiquette.

Helen's home was quite large with a lovely garden full of flowers and trees. Well, it certainly seemed large for a single lady. It added to his assumption that she wasn't short of a bob or two. 'Probably supported by her parents' he thought, 'but then maybe she had gained a lot of money, perhaps even the house, from the divorce settlement'. He did not feel that he should ask about things like that. He certainly did not want her to think he was after her money. That was certainly not the case and mentioning or probing those areas may make her think otherwise, so he just accepted the situation.

There were certain areas or subjects that he felt were best left alone. After all, he did not want to spoil their relationship for what may prove to be his own insecurity or show lack of trust in Helen. He remembered the questioning she put him through when they first met and the spooky, stalker-like, appearance outside of his house. There was also something he felt a little silly about. 'Why should that matter' he asked himself when he realised she wore her watch, especially with it being a wide cumbersome thing, in bed. 'You're being very trivial now' he castigated himself.

Apart from those events, he dismissed as trivial he decided there was one very important occurrence. In his words, it was, '**the** most important thing that I **must** challenge Helen about' as he mulled over their relationship. He thought 'Our sex life has just about everything going for it. But I find it disconcerting, to say the least, that Helen is always reluctant to dress or undress in front of me.' When they made love she would either, remain partly clothed, have the lights out or be already under the bedclothes. At first, he put it down to a little uncharacteristic shyness and thought it rather cute. As days turned into weeks and weeks into months he knew something was not right.

As he tried to unscramble in his mind the things that were bugging him he kept remembering others. For example, from time to time, it seemed as if she was holding something back. There had been times when she would be just about to tell him something yet was never forthcoming. She would suddenly turn very serious, say his name but then change the subject or distract him.

"Come on Helen spit it out," he jokingly encouraged her on one of those occasions.

"Hum, well, I..." she stumbled and stuttered with that serious look on her face as if she had something mind-blowingly important to say. *"Just, um, just....."* and then, as if what she was about to say had just come to her in a flash, with a bright uplift in her voice and demeanour she blurted, *"wondered if you would mow the lawn for me?"*

Perhaps this was just his imagination but he was as sure as he could be that she had not started the conversation with the intention of asking him to do something so mundane as to - *mow the lawn*.

Despite these things being of great concern to him he kept putting off saying or doing, anything that may cause the slightest of disagreement between them. Neil does not like confrontation and certainly did not want to be the one to trigger friction or anything that would jeopardise their, otherwise wonderful, loving relationship. So again his concerns were kicked into the long grass.

CHAPTER SEVEN: The Truth Hurts.

It was now 1965 and over the previous months, Neil had fallen, even more, head over heels in love with Helen. No one could replace Fiona and if it was possible he would have her back with him again in a trice. He held on to his belief that he would be reunited with her in heaven. He did not know what heaven would be like but he believed it would not have the same rules as earth and that everything would be fine. His thoughts were 'Thank God for God and the ability and intrinsic desire humans have to believe. To believe that this is not just an aimless life we lead with little or nothing to show for it at the end.'

Neil was visiting his sister Jenny back in Northallerton. They sat chatting over a cuppa and Neil was telling her about the latest date he had with Helen and his progress at her Dad's factory.

He had already broken the news some time ago that they were now in love. It was a little difficult because everyone perceives things in a different way and everyone reacts in a different way. He knew his sister well but there was still a little apprehension of how she would take it. After all his concern and soul searching he decided to take the plunge and phone her. However, his worry was unnecessary because Jenny just wanted what was best for Neil. She reconfirmed that today...

"I am really pleased you are doing so well now," said Jenny. *"You have met someone, fallen in love and found a new job."*

"Yes I am so lucky," remarked Neil.

*"**And**,"* continued Jenny, with a slight emphasis on the 'and' *"you seem almost back to your normal happy-go-lucky, chirpy self."*

"Chirpy, yes, that's the word my friendly newsagent once used to describe me. Yes, I suppose I am," confirmed Neil.

They chatted about lots of things that day catching up on local gossip and news.

"Before you go I have something to show you," said Jenny in a more serious tone. *"I have kept these; in fact, I have kept them **from** you and **for** you. I didn't show you them earlier because I haven't been too sure of your emotional state until recently and I really didn't think you should see them sooner."*

She took some slightly yellowing newspapers out of a drawer and opened them on the table. These were all the pictures and stories reported by the local newspaper of Neil and Fiona's accident on the 9th August 1961 and more covering the subsequent court case towards the end of October that year. There were photographs of all the people involved, obviously taken at some time before the accident occurred and offered by family and friends for publication. There was Fiona and Neil Collins; a little boy, Barry aged five, who died and his mother, the accused Mrs Mary Robinson, who was driving the Jaguar on that fateful day.

Neil felt he had to sit down, but took the cuttings with him.

"Sorry, perhaps I was wrong to show them to you after all," Jenny said softly seeing the effect it was having on her brother.

"No that's all right," answered Neil. *"I am glad you did. I just need a little time to read them and take it all in."*

"Shall I make us another cuppa?" Jenny asked thinking it best to give him some time and space.

Neil just nodded, smiled briefly and continued to stare at the pages. There was a picture of the cars after the accident. 'What a mess' he thought as he looked at the state of his car and the shattered windscreen on the Jaguar. Apparently, the child was on the back seat of the Jaguar when the cars collided and was not only catapulted through the front windscreen, the glass slashing deep onto his face and

104

body, but he also collided with what was left of the Morris Minor. He had died of his injuries and massive blood loss.

[Very few people in those days seemed to be bothered about **seat-belts**[9] only one or two determined motorists took it upon themselves to fit them DIY style.]

Although Barry had been in the back, considered the safest place, this was no protection from the ferocity of forces at play. Barry Robinson a good looking boy with fair hair and brown eye's stared back at Neil from the page. His picture was taken not long before his death. It showed a happy child with a cheeky smile and just a hint of mischief. Neil thought 'How sad.'

Neil's car was virtually unrecognisable. There was nothing left of the front nearside[10] where Fiona had been sitting. He could see that she did not stand a chance and that he was very lucky to be alive. 'It looks like I had time to turn the steering slightly to the right. What if I had, at that split second before the collision, turned the steering wheel the other way? It could have been a completely different outcome.' He did not know if the outcome would be better or just different. He did sometimes think it may have been better for Fiona but it was a long shot and no point now in dwelling on it. Though it was understandable why he did.

He eagerly, yet with a little dread, read the reports of the aftermath. The outcome of the court case put the blame completely and solely on Mary Robinson the driver of the Jaguar. She had already pleaded guilty of causing death by careless driving. The remorse she had shown and her guilty plea was acknowledged by the judge. So remorseful was she there were constant halts to proceedings. On one occasion a doctor had to be called. The judge also took into consideration that she had already paid a very high price for her actions having been responsible for her own son's death.

On top of that, she had also received life-threatening injuries from which she was still recovering. Her arm was in a sling and she was still attending the hospital outpatients department. These injuries were not as bad as Neil's but had she not been attended to very quickly, she too could have died from loss of blood. She was given a five year suspended prison sentence, fined £1,000 and banned from driving for five years.

Her only defence was that she was late for an appointment. She wasn't driving too fast but driving a little faster than usual and certainly had no time to stop to pay proper attention to her little boy. It had been a long drive from Newcastle and Barry started to get tired, bored and fidgety. Her son was travelling in the back seat but was playing up and threatening to climb over into the front. She had shouted to him to sit down. That did not work and as she turned to push him back onto the seat she was momentarily distracted. Also, the effort of pushing him and turning in her seat forced her right foot harder on to the accelerator and her right hand down on the steering wheel. Her actions caused the car to veer to the right across the road into the path of Neil's Morris Minor coming towards them.

Having been flung halfway through the front windscreen, Mary was also badly scarred across her face, head, back and her left wrist, suffered severe bruising along with a broken collar bone. Luckily for Neil and Mary a motorist caught up in the inevitable traffic jam was a doctor and was able to stem the flow of blood with the help of another person at the scene who knew first aid. Considering someone had to drive to the nearest telephone box to dial 999 the ambulance was on the scene very quickly and hospital staff were all extremely expert.

The two casualties who had a slim chance of survival actually made it through but Barry and Fiona died at the scene. Fiona had multiple injuries. Parts of the car had been forced through her body. The policeman in charge on the day reported that this was one of the worse scenes of carnage his officers and ambulance crew had ever had to deal with. Most of the really gruesome details were not reported in the papers. Still, this was stomach churning stuff for Neil to read, but read it he did, feeling he was compelled to. He sat for a while with his head in his hands. His emotion at this time was more bitterness than sadness.

There were very few pictures relating to the trial. The only one of Mary Robinson showed her leaving the court building with her head and face covered. 'Criminals all cover their face's' decided Neil and at that moment hated her with a great deal of venom. This was followed by a sudden pang of guilt for comparing her to a criminal when he read the next part of the report. Apparently, she was very self-conscious about her facial scars. To say that he had mixed feelings about this woman does not describe the complexity of his emotions. One moment she was a wife killer. Next, she was the victim of circumstance. Then he hated her and wished for vengeance. Then he felt a certain amount of sympathy after all she had also lost someone very dear to her and she, sure-as-shot, did not do that on purpose.

Seeing the pre-accident picture in the paper of Mary Robinson stirred up a feeling he could not explain. 'It is a little like déjà vu' Neil thought. He could not explain this. He certainly did not suffer from paramnesia[11].

He did not know the woman. To the best of his memory, he had never met her either before or since the accident. He had only ever seen her today in the newspaper yet she seemed to be, well let's say slightly, very slightly, familiar. 'Perhaps she was one of my customers at Smurthwaite's when I worked there as a mechanic. Although I don't seem to remember doing any work on a white Jaguar Mk X. No - I can definitely rule that idea out. First, hers was quite a new car and would be hardly likely to need any work. Secondly, she lives in Newcastle and it would be a long way to come for a service.' He decided 'She must just look a little like someone I have met before in my dim and distant past.' Neil never thought about it again.

He thanked Jenny for not only keeping the newspapers but for not showing them to him until now. He said, *"You were correct, I can cope with it now. It is always hard for me when I think about Fiona's death, it always will be, but I am more equipped to deal with it now. I can especially remember the good things and happy times we had without falling to pieces. Of course, I still have my moments. Although these moments of sadness will get fewer and further between, I don't think that they will ever leave me completely."*

"Yes I understand," replied Jenny. *"Send my regards to Helen and let's not leave it too long before we have another get-together."*

Neil agreed, they embraced and he set off back to Scarborough.

[The next morning, Neil's bedroom]

Neil woke up! As he laid there in his bed his eyes suddenly shot wide open, bulging like organ stops. This happened with a sudden realisation and *"No photographs!"* he murmured quietly as his body stiffened with tension.

Then, with a start, he sat bolt upright. It was like a dead man suddenly coming to life. His face as white as a sheet, his eyes even wider now and his jaw dropped, hanging as far as it would go. Trying to analyse, as he became properly awake, what it was that woke him up, he suddenly remembered. **"No photographs!"** he shouted and shot out of bed. He shot out and stood up so fast it caused him to go giddy and had to sit down again. The blood must not have had a chance to circulate around his brain properly, so fast was his rise to a standing position.

This morning was to be just like the start of any other day. Nothing special to do compared to any other day or so he thought when he went to bed. However all night, he seemed, sometimes to dream, sometimes to be half awake. The newspapers he read about the accident along with aspects of his new life kept whirling around in his head. Suddenly a revelation, which was strong enough to wake him up, jumped into his brain. He had not seen one photograph in Helen's house. Paintings of landscapes etc. yes but not one family photograph.

Ok - some people are not big on photographs especially those of family which can be a little boring and sometimes not do much for the decor of a room. What he could not understand is the lack of a photograph of her son. That was just beyond the realms of all reasoning. Neil thought he knew Helen at least well enough to know that she loved her son and it just did not make sense. Neil once noticed a child's cycle in Helen's shed. He remembers her saying 'It was his favourite toy. Even though I moved house, I just could not bear to get rid of it.' So he dismissed the idea that the child had died soon after or during birth. Furthermore what about the rest of her family? He knew she loved her father yet no picture? 'There is certainly something amiss here' he decided.

He knew nothing about Helen's son. Name, age, nor anything else, all this appeared to be taboo. Recovering from his giddiness he decided to calm down and play it cool. At the same time, he just knew that he would have to ask her about it. He and Helen had grown very close and he rightly assumed that by now she would have been able to confide in him or discuss sensitive and even hurtful subjects.

[Later at Helen's House]

"Hello darling," Helen took him in her arms as he entered the back door and kissed him as she often did. *"Do I detect a little lowering of the temperature?"* she asked, being conscious of a slightly less enthusiastic response than usual from her normally responsive lover.

"I am just a little tired today," replied Neil, *"I didn't sleep very well last night."* That was the truth but it was also an excuse to temporarily put off the looming confrontation. He took the opportunity to cast his eyes around the kitchen.

"You just go into the lounge and put your feet up. I'll pour you a nice glass of cool beer," offered Helen, *"and then I need to finish cooking this spaghetti."*

Neil thanked her and entered the lounge[12], although he did not sit down. As he entered, his eyes scanned the walls and the furniture tops, mantelpiece, sideboard etc. This was in order to make sure his revelation was right and that there was, indeed, no family photographs. He then popped his head around the kitchen door and made an excuse that he was going to the toilet. This, of course, was so he could quietly look into all the upstairs rooms and again nothing.

They sat in the dining room for their spaghetti bolognese and once more he found himself looking around.

*"You **are** tired,"* she observed, *"You seem as if you're in another world?"* she stated enquiringly as if at the same time, to ask why?

Neil was about to say something to, again, put off the moment of truth. Instead, pulling out all his tact and courage, he said, *"I have noticed you haven't any photographs of your son on display,"* he said quietly trying to sound nonchalant.

Helen did not answer immediately. There was quite a long pause when she said *"Ha well,"* but the expected explanation was not forthcoming. *"You see..."*

Neil waited and it looked like she was thinking hard. You could almost see and hear the cogs working. He waited a little longer and was just about to break the silence when she said. *"I am going to...... decorate. Yes, that's what I am going to do. I am going to decorate the whole house!"* Helen exclaimed. It was a eureka moment.

Now, this sounded to Neil, and I am sure you will feel the same, that Helen, just at that moment, decided to or perhaps we should say, just made up a story to decorate. It was not something that she had been planning or talking about before today. It had never even been mentioned in passing.

Neil thought about this and considering he did not remember seeing photographs on previous visits he found what she said impossible to believe. He decided she was lying, but he did not want to accuse her of such, so changed the subject. But this would not be the last of it by any stroke of the imagination. He just needed time to do a little bit of investigation.

[The following Saturday]

Saturday came and Neil was again at Helen's place. Saturday morning was their normal time for a shopping trip and their usual coffee in Spinetti's. They would go together but they were still buying for separate households.

"Would you mind going by yourself this morning love?" asked Neil. *"I am feeling a little hung over. I think I had a little too much to drink at the pub last night."*

"Really!" said Helen sounding surprised. *"I didn't notice. You seemed to be OK when I left you at your place."*

"You do not mind if I just curl up on the couch for an hour. I have taken a couple of Aspirins," said Neil. Ignoring Helen's disbelief, he continued, *"But I do have a couple of things I need at the shop if you would get them for me and I'll square up with you later?"* he asked, passing her a short shopping list.

"Oh! Bless you. You should have stayed at home if you weren't feeling well. I would have understood," as she took the list. *"Ok then see you soon,"* and off she went.

Now you're probably one step ahead here and have already realised that this was a ploy by Neil to be in Helen's house alone. He reasoned, 'if there were no photographs on the walls they must be stored somewhere.' You see he naturally did not believe that they did not exist. In fact, if Helen was telling the truth about decorating she was admitting there were photographs somewhere that had been removed from the walls in readiness. As soon as he had allowed time for her to catch the bus he started carefully looking through every drawer and cupboard in the house. He was careful to put things back as he found them because he did not want her to suspect anything at this stage.

He found nothing downstairs and seemingly nothing upstairs. He was just about to go back down. 'I know - the loft!' he thought. Just as he contemplated the struggle he would have getting into the loft through the very small and high opening he decided to check the wardrobes he had first dismissed. 'Photographs don't hang on rails and coat hangers,' he had at first decided, but something made him backtrack and open the wardrobe door in the main bedroom. Sure enough, there were shelves in it and cardboard boxes on those shelves.

He had soon found what he was looking for. Photo albums and frames all with pictures in. Although he had suspected something untoward was going on I do not think he was fully prepared for what he found.

He picked up a frame and turned it over. Staring back at him was the same good looking young boy that had stared back at him, with that mischievous smile, from the newspaper cuttings about the accident. Very shocked he realised 'This was Barry, Barry Robinson.' Neil thought for a while and asked himself. 'Why on earth has Helen got a picture of Barry Robinson?' A difficult question 'Hang on a minute. Unless...' There was a pause as he thought more deeply. 'Unless... Barry and Helen's son are, or were, one and the same. That would mean Helen must be... surely not.' Momentarily devastating thoughts ran through his mind then 'Don't be daft,' he told himself, 'Barry's mother was Mary Robinson.'

More determined now than ever to try to get some answers he grabbed the nearest photo album. Again more pictures of Barry but also lots of photographs of Mary. Well, Mary is certainly not Helen. One thing he was sure about, the Mary in the photographs was definitely the Mary who caused the accident. He stared at the next photo and was even more perplexed, it was Mary posing with pride beside her brand new white Jaguar Model Mk X.

Neil was really confused now and said to himself sarcastically. 'Helen must have a fetish for hoarding pictures of accident victims and perpetrators.'

Stunned and still confused he began to put the albums back. Just as he did that a loose photo fell from the back of the album. As he picked it up everything had either started to make sense or had got even more complicated, he did not know which. Neil had found perhaps the most surprising picture of all. It was of Mary Robinson and her father on the fifth anniversary of 'Crosby's' Aluminium Foundry owned by Ronald Crosby, **Helen's** father. Neil gathered that because on the back was written 'Me and dad, the fifth anniversary of the foundry.' Yet the photograph clearly showed Ronald Crosby with Mary Robinson.

As you know Neil worked for Crosby's so recognised Ron immediately. Neil's mind started to work overtime, 'could Helen have a secret sister called Mary?'

He stood not knowing what to think or what to do next. 'No' he said to himself. 'No, that is not possible.' He tried hard not even to allow himself to think of such a thing. 'Yet could it be, I don't know how Helen Crosby is really Mary Robinson?'

Although some things seemed to be clearer in his mind he was still left feeling more confused than ever. He did not know how to react perhaps it was too soon for any reaction.

What conclusion could he come to? Was his new love, really the woman responsible for Fiona's death? Was his new love the woman he once wanted to strangle? 'This cannot be!' he tried to convince himself. 'Although there seems to be conflicting evidence here in these photographs, I can see with my own eyes that she is not the same woman. When I look at Helen I do not see the woman in these photographs.'
He put that box away and started to look in other boxes. He was, he decided, coming to the end of his investigation as far as he could go today or so he thought.

"Waugh!" A strange noise of shock came from Neil's mouth. *"What have we here?"* He said out loud. He was almost knocked for six when a document he had found proved to be pivotal to his investigation.

"Waugh!" He reiterated very loudly this time *"This is the missing piece of the puzzle."* and thought 'Alas the proof I **did not** want to find.'

He held in his hand a file containing documents, photographs, letters and receipts for plastic surgery. Mary had undergone operations on her face. More stark realisations came to him. Things that at the time they occurred were unexplainable or unusual about Helen now started to become clear. Things he had thought trivial or had put to the back of his mind as being of little consequence were now dominant.
Questions, lots of questions, that had been the cause for concern now resurfaced. This time finally with answers.

He remembered the feeling of déjà vu when, at Jenny's house, he viewed the paper cuttings of Mary Robinson. It was her eyes, those big beautiful brown eyes; these were also the eyes of Helen Crosby. His mind went into overdrive trying to collate the information.

'Someone shouted at us when we went out for the day.' A flashback of their visit to York came to him. 'Some woman shouted Mary. I was convinced, despite Helen's strange reaction that it must have been a case of mistaken identity - but it wasn't. They say love is blind. How right they are.'

The resistance Helen showed against appearing, in front of him, fully naked. 'That was in order to hide scars. Probably the same reason for the very wide watch strap,' he decided.

The surgeons had done a very good job of hiding her facial scars and at the same time had changed her appearance at least enough for him not to immediately realise who she was. This may have been a natural event due to the operation or a purposeful effort to hide her identity, as well as her scars.

'The fact that Helen did not drive must be due to the driving ban.' Neil assumed again bringing to mind the newspaper article.

'This also solves the mystery of the flowers on Fiona's grave with the unsigned message, which read simply – 'So sorry'. They must have been left by Mary Robinson aka Helen Crosby.'

He now had answers to many of his questions, but there was one question, one big question which had only just occurred to him... 'Why?' ...'Why would a woman who had caused me such misery want to become my lover? Does she know who I am?' He asked himself and answered 'Well of course she does. She will have seen my picture in the paper and I have not changed my name or my appearance.'

Perhaps the more he discovered the more he needed to discover. 'Enough!' he was exhausted. 'Enough!' He packed everything away, all but one photograph, not worrying too much on this occasion about putting things back in the correct order.

His exhaustion was more mental than physical. He now also felt very let down, deceived and quite bruised. This woman who he had fallen in love with had led him up the garden path. Took his trust and at every opportunity hid the truth about who she was and what she wanted. 'What did she want?' he kept asking himself. 'I am not rich so she is certainly not after my money. If she was she would have been more inclined to marry me.' That did not make sense to him either. 'She has lots more money than me,' he concluded.

Neil had now had enough of beating about the bush, no longer was he going to play the softly, softly, approach. He wanted answers and he wanted them now. He waited for Helen's return. Hearing the back door being opened and closed he hid from view. Hiding in the front room still holding the photograph of Barry he stood up against the wall and was concealed behind the wide open door.

Helen crept into the house trying not to disturb Neil who she assumed may still be sleeping. Having slowly and carefully put away her share of the shopping and leaving Neil's in a separate bag on the draining board made her way quietly towards the lounge.

Neil could feel his heart pounding. It seemed so loud that she might be able to hear it. He held his breath as Helen tip-toed in. Seeing he was not on the couch she turned to her right, walking away from where

Neil was concealed, heading towards the hallway stairs thinking he may have gone to bed when...

"Mary!" a shout came from behind her. She stopped and stood still in shock.

To say Helen was shocked by hearing that name used is putting it mildly. She just froze not wanting to turn and face the truth.

"Mary!" the call from Neil came again; he violently kicked the door, slamming it shut, revealing his hiding place.

"Oogh!" she took a sudden and sharp intake of breath at the sound of the door slamming, then turned slowly towards him still frozen to the spot, speechless and starting to tremble.

*"That **is** your **real** name **isn't it Mary?**"* he said rather menacingly, getting closer and holding out the picture of Barry so she could see it. *"Please let me explain,"* she pleaded as she took the picture and laid it on the sideboard. She was soon interrupted.

"You certainly have a lot of explaining to do," Neil insisted as he grabbed her wrist and forcefully removed her watch. This, as he expected, revealed a scar. They both stood for a moment looking down at the scarred wrist. Helen looked back at him and half crying said...

"I know you must be angry but I did so hope that you would learn to love me despite it all. I meant to tell you everything but as time went by I lacked the courage and did not want to spoil what we had." She was now very frightened. She had never seen Neil look so fearsome. His upper lip was tightening and lifting, showing one side of his upper teeth, almost animal-like. His eyes seemed to be on fire and every vein in his neck stood out. His fists were tightly clenched one of them still around her wrist.

"Please," she pleaded. *"You're hurting me."*

"Me hurting you?" He yelled. *"Do you realise how much you have hurt me.* ***You killed my wife, you nearly killed me, you deceived me, and you have lied to me time after time. Are you the devil?"***
As you know Neil has never been one for violence. He realised that he was starting to lose control. He had to get out of there before he did something both of them would regret.

Helen was now crying prolifically.

He threw her arm back at her pushing her on to the floor and for a moment stood over her cowering figure like a gladiator about to deliver the fatal blow.

Never before had he been so furious. His blood pressure was probably through the roof. His face and eyes were red with blood-filled veins. His tongue snake-like as each spoken word appeared to be accompanied by a spray of venom.

His parting shot was like a spear being driven time and time again through Helen's heart. Prodding his finger, dagger-like, towards her and his face contorting in hatred with every syllable, he shouted slowly and very deliberately...

"I never, ever, want to see you, again!"

With that, he stormed out, grabbed the bag of shopping on the way, and slammed the door behind him. He didn't bother to check that the shopping was his. He just wanted to get as far away as possible as quickly as possible.

Helen simply lay on the floor crying. She was hurting badly. Neil had done no physical harm to her other than a bruised wrist where he had held her very tightly. She was expecting more. 'I deserve to be punished' she said to herself, thoughtfully, expecting to have received much more than a bruised wrist.

The hurt she was suffering was much worse than physical pain. Her insides were bleeding mentally. She chastised herself for not having come clean much sooner in the relationship. The agony of her whole life now seemed to bear down upon her. It wasn't just today's drama that caused her to sob uncontrollably but the baggage of sorrow and desolation she carried with her; the miscarriage, Molly's death, Barry's death, her divorce and now the loss of her lover.

'I am done now' she thought, 'I am lost. I feel so hopeless, helpless and worthless.'

She managed to make her way to the bedroom and cried herself to sleep.

Meanwhile, Neil had got home, dropped the shopping on the floor, grabbed a bottle of beer from the fridge and collapsed crying onto the couch. ***"How could she?"*** he cried out loud and sobbed into his beer. There was no consoling him. There was no one there to console him but even if there had been there was still no consoling him.

He spent the evening going over and over everything in his head. He was so tired because it had all taken so much out of him he eventually fell asleep on the couch where he lay.

CHAPTER EIGHT: What Now?

Monday morning came around as Monday mornings do though for Neil this was no ordinary Monday morning. It was the beginning of another week, but this time, without Helen and without a job. He decided not to go to work. 'I cannot imagine Helen's, or is it Mary's, dad wanting to see me again' he convinced himself. 'After all, he must have been in on it so I don't think I want to see him again either.'

What now then? He had picked himself up before, can he do it again? 'Yes,' he said to himself 'I will go for a run like I used to before I started full-time work and buy a paper to see if there is anything going on the job scene.'

Most of this was really a brave front. How he was feeling inside was not represented by the words in the last two paragraphs. He was near to breaking point. He was far from positive and was pushing himself all the way. What had just happened to him was very traumatic. He had put so much thought into a new relationship and once it was consummated put so much trust in the person he regarded as his new lifetime lover, companion, friend and soul mate. He was, in fact, grieving all over again.

When he got back with his newspaper he had just got through the door when the phone began to ring.

"Is that Neil?" asked a familiar sounding voice from the other end of the phone.

"Yes, who's that?" answered Neil. Whilst he suspected who it was, he didn't believe his ears, but it definitely was his boss. Expecting an ear bashing Neil was just about to go on the defensive when he heard a very friendly and polite tone say...

"Look I know about you two falling out..." Falling out! - that must be the understatement of the year. *"... I do not really want to get involved but I have*

phoned for two reasons. One, I was very much against what my daughter was doing and constantly pressed her to tell you who she really was. Secondly, your job is still here if you want it. You are a good worker and I have further plans for you and my foundry which, if it all works out, would mean your promotion. This is purely on merit and nothing to do with your relationship with my daughter. What do you say? Are you in or out?"

"In!" answered Neil without needing to give it a second thought and added, *"Thank you very much indeed."*

"I expect to see you tomorrow morning then, bye," and with that put the phone down.

Mr Crosby was always very businesslike, sometimes appearing to be stern and always forthright and straight to the point, but always looked after his staff and Neil did get on well with him. Neil needed the job and was delighted, 'Things had already started to go right.' He again tried to be positive despite the heavy heart he carried.

He naturally started to put his mind to the situation with Helen. The one big question that had not been answered was WHY?

During the following days, he tried to get back to life as it was before Helen. He had managed before he can manage now was his philosophy. It was quite a near escape he thought. 'I was actually thinking of marrying her.' He shook his head at the thought.

He could not get back completely to a 'without Helen' life because he owed his job to Helen. Also, he could not stop thinking about her and why she did it - he wanted answers. He knew what she had done, and to a great extent how she had done it, but he did not know why.

Wanting to know 'why' soon took over his life. When he wasn't working he just could not seem to stop thinking about it. He tried once while at work to broach the subject with Helen's dad but Mr Crosby made it quite clear, again, that he did not want to get involved and would not discuss it with him.

"You really need to ask her," was Ron's only helpful remark. Yes, by now, he was on first name terms with Ronald Crosby.

Neil picked up on this advice. As he sat there in his flat mulling over his options, there was really only one. So coming to a conclusion he said to himself. 'There is only one way I am going to find out why and that is to ask her'. Whilst he had made it plain to her, at the time, that he never wanted to set eyes on her again, he decided that he would see her, if she would see him, just one more time.

Daunting though it seemed he realised that meant arranging a meeting. It needed to be somewhere neutral, perhaps the cafe, where they had their first coffee together and had visited and drunk coffee together many times since. He realised that the meeting would have to be a calm relaxed discussion. No raised voices, no nastiness or recriminations. He would have to be prepared to just listen intently and actively with little or no emotion or he may never know why she went through all that deceit and cover-up over all that time.

He went round to her house without her expecting him. He did not want to phone because people can hang up on you. He did not really expect Helen to do that but he decided not to take that chance.

Luckily she was at home but quickly half closed the door again when she saw it was Neil.

"It's OK," He reassured her, "I have calmed down now." He realised she was afraid he would be aggressive again.

Helen took heart and relaxed as she thought 'Neil is not likely to do anything to jeopardise his job.' That and his present calm demeanour allowed her to feel more at ease so she opened the door a little wider.

"I want some answers, I think you owe me that," said Neil still calmly but firmly.

"Do you want to come in?" she asked.

"No!" straight to the point and sounding a little sterner he added, *"And don't think that I am here for any other reason than to get some answers. I don't want you to get the wrong idea. Can you meet me in the cafe on Saturday morning at about ten o'clock?"*

"Yes sure," answered Helen knowing exactly which cafe he meant and with that, he was gone.

[Spinetti's cafe the following Saturday]

Helen made sure she was there in plenty of time so that she did not have the embarrassment of discussing who was going to pay for the coffees or where they should sit etc. She paid for her coffee and a round of toast and sat down at the table in the corner furthest away from other customers. She had not eaten breakfast that morning as her stomach was turning and churning from the moment she awoke. She could still feel the butterflies doing their worst but thought she ought to try and eat something. 'Not a good idea to face this on an empty stomach.' She decided. The last thing she wanted was to start feeling faint. She was going to need to stay strong and clear headed.

She had practised what she was going to say over and over again. The only trouble is it had been practised in many different ways and she really did not know how it would sound best. She made her mind up that it was certainly going to be the truth and from the heart. 'Perhaps it is a good thing that I have not learned it like a script.' She agreed with her own reasoning. 'That would sound very false even though it's all going to be the truth.'

Now that Neil knew who she was, she actually felt like a slave who had just been given their freedom. Now she thought, 'I am free, to tell the truth, the whole truth, and nothing but the truth.' Then she realised 'That sounds as if I will be in the dock all over again.' It sent a shiver through her body when she realised that was just how it might be. Her appearance in court and how she felt standing in the dock flashed through her mind. Even now she was still suffering from the effects of that day. 'A few fleeting seconds' she digressed, 'of distraction from my driving has caused loss of life for some and for me and everyone else involved what seems like a lifetime of misery and heartache.'

Whilst she was naturally partly very anxious, she was also very glad that, as far as Neil was concerned, she was now completely free of the shackles of her past. No more lies, no reason for deceit, no more having to hide herself or her identity.

Neil walked into the cafe with a very brisk businesslike stride. He acknowledged Helen with the smallest nod he could manage that could still be seen and yet not look too friendly. Without breaking his stride he went straight to the counter to purchase his drink. *"Coffee, please Luigi."*

"Yes-a sir. Frothy?" came the reply 'As if I-a needed, to ask-a' thought Luigi as Neil answered, *"Yes please."*

Neil sat opposite Helen as far away as he could without being on the next table and yet still near enough to reach and stir his coffee. He would not have been there or anywhere near her if it wasn't for his overwhelming desire to know why she had done what she had done. Now he must focus on the two questions he needed to find a definitive answer to. One: Why she acted out this panoply of lies and deceit? Two: Can he trust, what Helen tells him today will be the truth? After all, she has a very poor record on that score.

He continued stirring his coffee much more and for much longer than any drink would ever need. Helen looked directly at him wishing things were different. For despite everything she loved him. Oh yes, there must be no doubt in the reader's mind. She loved him and knew that this meeting was going to be her make or break chance to redeem herself. A huge task though she realised it was.

Apart from the noise of the stirring spoon, there was a long silence. Every other distraction, chatter from customers and clatter of plates etcetera was not heard by either Neil or Helen. It was as if the whole world was waiting to see what was going to happen.

Suddenly the spoon stopped. Neil looked directly at Helen and said pointedly and finishing his last word with a deep sigh of exasperation and a drooping of his head.

"I just want to know W H Y?"

"Where shall I begin?" Helen, knowing exactly what he meant, echoed his sighing voice, with almost the same sense of exasperation.

"At the beginning would be a good place," suggested Neil sarcastically.

Helen inhaled, filling her lungs with air and began. *"I know it does not appear so, and I can understand why you would perceive things differently but **why** I did this is all about my love for you."* She felt very proud, though a little shocked, at the eloquent way in which she had delivered the first line. This gave her the courage she needed to press on. *"So the **big why** is very simple. I love you. I love you very dearly."* At which point she kept quiet fully expecting Neil to deliver a tirade of scepticism and vector of disbelief. Nothing happened; he simply took another sip of his coffee. *"You know I rather expected you to jump down my throat at this point,"* said Helen, obviously very surprised.

Neil put down his cup, moved his chair a little closer to the table and said quietly and reassuringly but very deliberately. *"You know - I am not a violent person, yet I was sorely tested on the day I found out who you really are, how you deceived me and how many lies you told. It caused me a great deal of pain and terrible provocation. On many occasions over the years, I have wanted to strangle Mary Robinson or do her some other great harm. Yes! I admit it - I did sometimes feel I wanted to take violent revenge. So, not only did I have a score to settle for Fiona's death but you had also added insult to injury by hiding the truth. Furthermore like a Venus Fly-Trap you lured me in unsuspectingly and made me love you. Then .... there you were, lying vulnerable in front of me, at my mercy. Despite my furious anger and the temptation being so great, I left your house rather than take a chance that I would do something very out of character."*

The reliving of that moment seemed to sap the strength from Neil and make him tense up. He paused and willed himself to relax, took another drink of coffee and continued.

"I promised myself that I would stay calm today and listen. I will only say something if absolutely necessary perhaps to ask a question. If I am going to have my questions answered I need to allow you to tell me your story, without being interrupted and without fear of any adverse reaction." He paused briefly then said, *"Please carry on."*

Helen sensed the gradual build of tension as he spoke. Then realised he was now calm again and willing to listen. Helen had nothing to fear now so continued to tell her story and spoke with even more courage.

"I didn't love you at first. I felt sorry for you but to be honest just after the accident the person I felt most sorry for was myself. I know you went through a great deal of pain and I am quite aware that the accident and death of your wife was my fault. I took and I still take full responsibility, but you need to bear in mind that I too have been through a lot of agonies." She began to elaborate.

"I had already lost my first two children. First through miscarriage then my second child, Molly, died in my womb and was still born." Neil knew nothing of this. *"Then I was faced with the stark truth that I had killed my own son."* Speaking so bluntly made her heart heavy and her eyes fill up. 'No, no, I must not let this happen' she thought fighting back the tears. She needed to be strong to ensure Neil got the full story.

Pulling herself together she continued *"I was also responsible for the death of a stranger. I almost died and was left disfigured. I was now a criminal with a prison sentence hanging over me and a police record. It did not stop there. My husband blamed me, quite rightly, for Barry's death but could not come to terms with the situation and it caused the breakdown of our marriage. Our marriage and complete family, as Jeff called it, that we had both worked so hard through great adversity to achieve was finished. Losing Barry destroyed him."* She stopped to choke back the tears.

"I know for a fact that Barry's death was the reason Jeff no longer wanted me. The other thing, although he never admitted it, was my scarred face. The woman he had married was no longer the woman he saw in front of him, except perhaps my eyes. Thankfully they escaped damage.

Fighting even harder now to keep the tears at bay and dabbing her eyes with her handkerchief. *"I had lost everything, my son, my looks, my good name and my husband. If it wasn't for my father standing by me, morally, affectionately and financially, I would also have lost my sanity and perhaps the will to live."*

She had to pause again as if needing to regain strength. All this time Neil was trying, with difficulty, not to be affected by her tale of trauma. He did his best to regain his composure immediately the slightest look of sympathy or concern showed in his face.

Helen had a good long drink of coffee as if to take the strength from it that she needed to carry on. *"I went through hell. Every time I looked in the mirror I was reminded of my ugliness and the accident. Then there were the people who pointed at me in the street. I did not know whether they were saying, there's that murderer or look at that ugly woman."* She paused then added, *"Probably both."* She paused again then, *"One passerby even shouted,* **'child murderer'** *which was the hardest to bear."*

Almost pleading to get some reaction from the inscrutable Neil, she leant closer to him and asked with her voice breaking up, *"Can you imagine what that was like?"*

Quite shocked and certainly caught off guard at being asked his opinion Neil replied.
"Err, no, no, err, yes, I mean, I'm sorry," and took another swig of coffee to try to hide his obvious sympathy and embarrassment at his less than coherent and half-hearted answer.

Helen went on, *"Like you, I am usually quite a positive person although circumstances had knocked a lot of that out of me. Anyway, I decided to do something about it. I would take positive steps to make the best of the rest of my life. Someone somewhere once said,* **'don't let the bastards grind you**

down' *and when that phrase came into my mind I became determined to do what I could to put things right. I knew it would not happen overnight but I straight away made a start."*

Helen thought for a while to get things in the correct order in her mind then carried on. *"With my dad's help, I arranged to have plastic surgery at least on my face. I dyed my hair. I used to be a light sort of mousy brown colour so I decided to go dark brown. My full married name was Mary Helen Robinson so I reverted to my maiden name, Crosby and dropped the Mary. The final part of my rehabilitation was to move house. That didn't happen straight away. There were problems with the terms of the divorce etc. I am glad it was delayed because I finally decided to move to Scarborough."*

"What made you move here?" asked Neil, with genuine interest and concern. He felt a little bit awkward that he had not allowed himself to show any emotion. He was moved by her story and was warming to her.

"Once I had got myself more or less sorted out I did realise that there were some things I could not put right. I could not bring my son back and could not give you back your wife. What I could do though was track you down and try to help you financially. I am not a millionaire but I sort of got the idea that you were, well, shall we say, not that well off. I just wanted to help. Can I get you another coffee?"

"I'll get them." Neil jumped up, *"Usual?"*

"Yes please," She was so glad that the sternness had gone out of Neil's voice and although the atmosphere was far from normal she sensed that some of his angst, underlying bitterness and anger directed at her had dissipated.

Putting a couple of spoons of sugar into his cup Neil smiled and said, *"Somehow I don't think this coffee will need quite as much stirring."*

Helen chuckled and felt so pleased that the ice was starting to break. She just kept her fingers crossed metaphorically that they would both be lovers again after this heart to heart was over.

Neil gave Helen a gentle reminder as to where she was in her story, *"You were saying that you wanted to help me and had tracked me down."* He definitely wanted to hear the rest.

"Oh yes!" she remembered, almost burning her lips on the hot coffee. *"Mmm, oow, that's hot, err, yes that's right, well I hired a private detective to do that. I would like to be able to say that I moved here just because of you, but that isn't the case. When I found out where you were, coincidently, I liked this neck of the woods. Also, I was closer to my father's home, and factory, so that was another bonus. I am renting the house at the moment with an option to buy it."*

Neil interrupted. He was a little confused that she knew where he was but did not know where he lived it seemed a contradiction. *"How come you did not know where I lived when you had a private investigator working for you?"*

"It turned out that the private investigator had not done such a good job," explained Helen. *"He got the street right but had given me the wrong house number. I realised that when I knocked on, what turned out to be, someone else's door who had never heard of you. Then I resorted to beachcombing having been told where you exercise most mornings. I didn't, well I couldn't, knock on every door. Yours is a very long road."*

They both started to smile because it reminded them of when Helen had appeared across the street from Neil's house. Having followed him from the beach that morning, she returned in the afternoon to continue looking for him. She was spotted looking, by chance, directly into his window, as she pondered her next move.

"Even from that first time we met on the beach, remember when you thought I was rather weird because of the way I stared at you as I passed close by," she went on, *"I had fallen in love with you. Most of what appears to have been deceitful acts, by hiding things from you about me and my past, was because of love at first sight.*

I fell head over heels in love with you and that changed everything. No longer was I there just to try and help you and in some small way make recompense. I had planned all along to tell you the truth fairly soon after getting to know you and originally it did not matter to me if you still hated me. If you did not want to know me I would have accepted that. In fact, I half expected it. I thought about putting some money directly into your bank account anonymously but I was also doing these things for my own peace of mind and needed at least to try for your forgiveness. You could have sent me packing with a flea in my ear and although I would have been a bit sad about it, it would have made very little difference. At least I would have known that I had tried to do what I thought was the right thing."

For a second time, she turned to him and said, *"Can you imagine what that was like?"* This time she did not wait for a reaction but went on to say, *"If I told you who I was and why I was there, too soon, I would surely have been taking a big risk of losing you. I did not know how things would turn out. I did not know for sure that you would love me in return, but I just could not risk doing anything that may jeopardise what could be my last chance of love."*

They were both very engrossed. Helen in telling the story, Neil in listening and weighing up what he was hearing. He had to make sure that what he was being told was the truth. Did this woman sitting in front of him really love him?

Having neglected their coffees, they both took this lull in proceedings as an opportunity, almost in unison, to have a drink. Together they placed the cups back into their saucers and Helen resumed her dialogue.

*"So whilst I did not set out to deceive, if I wanted to hold on to you, I had no choice. I did lie to you the day you caught up with me on the bus. I said I **liked** you. That was not true, I **loved** you. I lied when we sat in this very cafe and I said I was happy to be a friend. My feelings for you were always much more than that of a friend. My constant very strong wish to come clean was always overpowered by my stronger desire, never to lose you. I often started to tell you the truth but always chickened out. Of course, I never did offer you money, as was my original plan, that was no longer appropriate but I did find ways to help like putting a word in for you with my dad about the job. He really does rate you very highly and always advised,*

in fact, constantly urged me to tell you everything, yet at the same time insisted he was not going to get involved."

There was a long pause. Helen thinking 'Have I left anything out?' Neil thinking 'Is there more to come?'

"That is my story, how we have ended up here." She stretched out her hand to lay it on top of his, but his hand was immediately retracted. Helen had started to feel good but this latest rebuttal brought her back down to earth. Did his reaction to her touch mean there was no way of healing this wound between them? She spoke again, *"I am so sorry that you had to find out in the way you did. I hope you can forgive me. I do not want to lose your love."* Helen did understand that it was a lot for him to take in and perhaps she was wrong to expect any outward sign of affection for her so soon.

Neil said nothing just stared down at the table where his hand had been. 'How can I love the woman who killed Fiona?' he thought, 'How can I give my life to the woman who took away the most precious gift in the world?' He appeared to be mulling things over in his mind and Helen thought it wise to shut up and stay quiet now. She had been given the chance to speak and Neil had been true to his word and had listened quietly and intently to what she had to say. It was only right to give him time to digest it.

He knew deep down that he had accepted her explanation. He also knew deep down she was a woman he could, did or should love. He was very unsure of his feelings. One thing he was very sure about and determined to make this thought his final one 'It would be a complete betrayal of my love for Fiona if I allowed myself to love Helen.'

He felt absolutely certain that Fiona would have been happy for him to move on and have a wonderful life finding somebody new to share it with. But surely, **not with the woman who took her life!!**

With that last thought still ringing in his ears like a loud bell, he rose slowly from his chair looking down directly into Helen's eyes. These big brown eyes were again slightly moist and her face filled with hope and expectation. Neil said to her gently but meaningfully. *"I have listened to you very carefully and I want you to know that I believe you. I also want you to know that I forgive you and I mean;* **I forgive you for <u>everything</u>."**

Helen could control herself no longer and the tears of sheer happiness poured forth. Whilst there were tears, you could see the joy in her face. Her eyes glowed and her face shone. Neither she nor Neil seemed to notice but people had started to look at them. Luigi, the owner, was keeping an eye out, aware that something seemed to be disturbing his customers.

Helen's relief of forgiveness from Neil was tremendous. Thinking everything was going to be fine had made her cry with relief. She had so longed for his forgiveness and finally, it had happened.

Neil could feel his emotions welling up. Seeing Helen's reaction made it even harder for him and he knew he just had to go. Neil held his hand out towards Helen for a formal handshake. She did not understand what was happening, or why his face was quite grim, but automatically stood up and put her hand in his. Neil continued. *"I wish you well and hope you have a good life. I just know there is some lucky man out there whose life will be made complete when he finds you, but for us this is goodbye."*

Neil could tell she did not want to let go. Her face had gone grey with the shock and her tears of happiness were now tears of great sadness. Neil managed to pull his hand free then made a quick exit. He felt bad about leaving her like that but knew there was no other way.

She watched unbelievingly as the man she loved disappeared, not just from view but from her life. She slumped back into her chair virtually collapsing on to the table knocking over the cups and wept loudly. She just could not control her emotions. The tears poured as if the walls of a dam had cracked or a river had burst its banks. People around were obviously disturbed by all this commotion but decided to leave her alone, at least for a while. However, Luigi came over and asked her,

"Are-a you OK?" A silly question but what else can you do in situations like that? She was inconsolable and continued to wail out loud.

They had used that cafe a lot and Luigi knew they were good customers. He was very kind and thoughtful, almost starting, without knowing why, to shed a tear himself.

"Silly, silly," he said quietly of himself, feeling exactly that, a bit silly, and quickly removed any sign of emotion from his face.

He stayed with her until she had pulled herself together. Not that she felt 'together' far from it. Helen had fallen apart and Luigi had to phone her dad, on her behalf, to come and collect her. Ronald Crosby had to help his daughter to, and into, his car as she could hardly manage to walk due to the trauma of it all.

CHAPTER NINE: Crosby's Christmas Party.

A few months later and Neil had still not made peace with himself. He was still having second thoughts about how he handled his meeting with Helen at the cafe. He felt guilty after hearing through the grapevine what her response had been after he left. He did not want to phone her or ask her father how she was. He did not want anyone, particularly Helen, to think he was trying to get back with her.

He naturally hoped she was OK now and was recovering. He realised that perhaps he was also still recovering. He had been strong to resist her affections but thought it right and proper that he had taken the stand he did. There were times of course when he wasn't so sure, and put that down to moments of weakness.

One Sunday, Neil went to church. He was not a regular attendee and often played war with himself for not going often enough. Before Fiona's death, he did go with her regularly to their local church in Northallerton, almost every Sunday. He wasn't one of these people who blamed God for everything, and Fiona's death was not the reason he stopped going. Going to church was something he had always done and he continued to share the habit with Fiona. What with moving, and all that, he just got out of the habit. 'There is never a wrong time to go' he thought and realised that he urgently needed some spiritual input.

As he neared the church he noticed that its tower was very similar in shape to All Saints where he was married. He looked closely and could see the clock and above and to one side of that the slatted louvre windows which allow the sound of the bells to come out but stop the rain getting in. It was just coming up to nine o'clock. As it was more a spur of the moment decision to come to church he did not know what time the service started. He often woke early so getting there for nine o'clock, just in case, was no problem. The service said the sign at the door, actually started at ten. So he decided to wander around looking at the architecture and reading the gravestones. This was St Mary's, in

the direction of Scarborough Castle. It was not too far from his flat for someone as fit as Neil that is.
One particular headstone that caught his attention across Church Lane was at the grave of Anne Bronte. The headstone was very weathered and difficult to read. Evidently, she was the youngest of the three Bronte sisters who wrote novels. Charlotte Bronte had brought her sister Anne to Scarborough in the hope that the sea air would cure her illness.

As he walked back to the church he could see that part of the original older building was missing with just a few ruins remaining. They had built the new wall and just left the remains as they were. He learned later that the east end and north transept of St Mary's had been destroyed by supporters of the King during the civil war in 1645. History tells us that the Parliamentarians had set up their guns in the Sanctuary of St. Mary's, firing at the Castle above them and the return fire from the King's supporters caused the damage.

The time, unusually, seemed to go quickly for Neil who soon found himself entering this new church, well new to him. 'What an impressive building' he decided. The carvings the stained glass and many artefacts intrigued him. The huge pillars 'much stouter than those in All Saints Parish Church back in Northallerton' he decided. 'They must have run out of money or stone' he thought when noticing some of the stone arches seemed unfinished.

He had listened to the words of the prayers, he prayed for others including Fiona, Helen and Jenny. He also prayed for himself and had some quiet thinking time before the service started. He joined in robustly with the hymn singing. He wasn't the best singer but did enjoy a good sing song, and managed to remain in tune most of the time.

He knew that some non-churchgoers would mistakenly think that Christians believed themselves to be goody-goodies. On the contrary, Neil and most Christians he knew went because they needed it and knew they needed it. Having faith had helped him cope with the death of loved ones he lost as a child and the loss of Fiona. Also with his own brush with death 'Now,' he confirmed to himself, 'was the right time to start going again.'

He felt at ease in there. Most of the people seemed happy, mind you like most churches he had been in, some of the congregation needed to tell their faces. Others were happy and friendly with smiling faces and when he came in greeted him with *"Hello or good morning."*

Some members of the congregation shared the peace with him. This is the time during the service where the vicar repeats the words Jesus said when he greeted his disciples, *"Peace, be with you."* Then each member of the congregation would turn to the next, shake their hand and also greet them with, *"Peace, be with you."*
He noticed, as happened in his original church there were one or two people just going through the motions, looking past you over your shoulder for the next person while shaking your hand and not fully recognising the importance of the process.

Neil was aware of how easy it is to slip into that bad habit and always made sure to give each person a few dedicated moments of his time. The person in front of him was the most important person. He looked directly into their eyes and greeted them clearly and sincerely.

It had been a long time since he had taken communion and this really did feel satisfying. He had always felt that Jesus was his friend and was able to pray to him and talk with him whenever and wherever life took him. He also realised how important taking communion was, so whilst eating the bread and drinking the wine he said to himself and to God that he would definitely be back again next week.

As you can tell Neil is no bible basher. There have been few references to his faith previously but his personal relationship with Jesus was very important to him. When, at times, he had seemed very alone. When it seemed that everyone around him had let him down or when he had let himself down. The one person that was always there for him was Jesus.

There was never any visions or booming voices, speaking to him out of the heavens. He just believed that if he put his problems into the hands of Jesus, they would be easier to endure and sometimes solved. He decided long ago to take that step of faith and believe his friend Jesus was there for him with unconditional love.

He was quite aware of what faith meant. It did not mean knowing for sure, categorically. It meant believing without categorical proof. There was one thing he was categorically sure about. If, perhaps, after death, he found that his Christian beliefs were all false he would still be thankful for the faith he had. It is now, on Earth, today, in the present, he needed Jesus, while he was alive.

He quite enjoyed the service even though the sermon did seem to go on a bit. As he came out into the fresh air he remembered, when he used to go to church before with Fiona in Northallerton, he always felt better for going. That is how he felt today. It seemed to recharge his batteries. He walked home with a spring in his step.

[A few days before Christmas 1965]

Neil had very mixed feelings about going to Crosby's Christmas Party. He did his best to think of ways to get out of it without success. He was a key player in the factory now. Not quite the boss's right-hand man but not far off. A lot of people expected him to be there, including Ron himself who would have been very disappointed, to say the least, if Neil had not turned up.

It will be fairly obvious why he wanted to back out. Yes, that's right, he fully expected Helen to be there. He had gone out of his way to avoid her for months and once momentarily left the factory through the back door when he caught sight of her entering via the front.

He often pondered what was behind this evasion. Having read the story so far you may assume that he was still angry with her. 'Am I still angry?' he thought 'Do I still hold a grudge? Well, Neil was not sure either. 'Is it the awkwardness of the situation?' He felt sure there was certainly a bit of that. 'What would I say to her after such a long time and after the way we parted?'

Then he recalled the way they parted. He whispered to himself a repeat of those last words.

"I wish you well and hope you have a good life. I just know there is some lucky man out there whose life will be made complete when he finds you, but for us this is goodbye."

He remembered it word for word. It had been emblazoned on his memory. He was also very conscious of not contacting her or asking after her when he found out how devastated she was. He did not dare to let her think that he was backtracking.

'That's it' he thought and started talking to himself out loud. *"Be honest, that's why you would rather not go to the party. You subconsciously want to backtrack. You know she has hardly been far from your thoughts."* His thoughts had not all been about the deception or the blame she accepted for Fiona's death. He had forgiven her for that. A lot of the time his mind was filled with the many moments of happiness he had shared with Helen and how in different circumstances they would still be together. Going back to the last words he spoke to her he often wished that he could be that *'lucky man'* out there whose life was made complete.

[The night of the party Saturday 18th December 1965]

All dressed up in his dinner suit and bow tie because this was quite a posh Christmas party, Neil arrived at the Grand Hotel in Scarborough. He was not really in the sort of mood for partying. He wasn't what you would call sad he just wasn't looking forward to the inevitable and imminent meeting with Helen. 'Let's just hope it's brief and painless' he thought as he alighted from the taxi.

Neil's flat was not all that far away from the Grand Hotel but the taxi was paid for by the company and 'just as well' he thought, as he did not intend to drive and he decided, 'the weather is a bit bleak for walking especially in my best clobber.'

"Merry Christmas," he wished the taxi driver as he reached back into the cab and pressed a shilling into his hand. He was trying to get into the Christmas spirit and after all, if he had had to pay for the taxi it would have cost him a lot more than that.

He climbed the steps under the Romanesque arch of the main entrance with its rose-coloured Italian marble pillars and passed through the foyer which opened out into, what can best be described as, an intricate, elaborately decorated and very magnificent reception room. 'The Grand Hotel has certainly been named well.' He thought as he surveyed the pillars, arches, sculptures and the very impressive staircase which lead to several floors with balcony landings. 'It feels grand' he said to himself 'Not only does this building dominate, on the outside, the South Bay of Scarborough from its position on St. Nicholas Cliff but the inside of the building makes me feel very special' as he again scanned and marvelled at the work that had gone into the building's interior.

He was very happy with the venue, which he had been meaning to check out ever since visiting the area all those years ago with Fiona. He decided, 'Anyway, if it is good enough for Sir Winston Churchill,' who was reported to have stayed at the Grand on several occasions, 'then it is certainly good enough for me.'

Realising where the sound of partying and music was coming from, he made his way to the ballroom. There was Ron in the doorway greeting his staff as they arrived. Neil shook hands and greeted the boss, swapped pleasantries and then moved on to talk to several of his workmates and colleagues as he made his way through the packed ballroom. Whilst Ron's Foundry did not employ hundreds of people Ron had very kindly invited the wives and husbands free of charge and agreed that each could bring two friends providing they paid a nominal contribution towards the cost. This, he said, *"Was in the spirit of the season and would give his staff more opportunity to enjoy the evening."*

Neil's eyes were immediately drawn to this radiant female figure in a stunning red dress, standing in the furthest away corner of the room, obviously enjoying a drink and chatting with other party goers. It was Helen. His eyes had been drawn to her immediately, and although there were obviously many people in the room it was as if she was the only person in existence. She was pinpointed on his radar and immediately captured his gaze which remained focused on this elegant figure. For a while, he stood motionless just staring. People spoke to him in greeting and went to shake his hand but there was no response, he did not even know they were there.

"Eh! Fella, are you OK?" asked Bob, the factory security man, as he stood in front of Neil and took him by the elbows, as if about to give him a shake.

"Oh!" Neil came back to his senses *"Yes, sorry Bob! I was in a world of my own there for a minute. How are you doing?"*

"I am just fine thank you, but more to the point, how are you? You certainly looked a bit glassy-eyed there for a moment. I thought I was going to have to use my first aid skills," he said, chuckling to make light of it, yet at the same time, he was quite serious.

"Sorry, I think I must have a cold coming on or something," was the only excuse Neil could think of on the spur of the moment.

"Well, you take care, Neil. See you later," and with that, he was off to mingle.

Neil made his way to the bar. Choosing a spot furthest from the place he had seen Helen standing. After waiting some time to get served ordered a pint of Newcastle Brown and sat at a table with a few of the people he worked closest with at the factory. He discussed with them everything from the weather to the latest NASA space mission. Evidently, the latest news of their ventures was that on the 15th just gone Gemini 6 had manoeuvred in space to within one foot of Gemini 7, the very first rendezvous of two craft in space.

"I wouldn't be surprised if they land a man on the Moon before too long," remarked Neil before his mind started to wander on to other things.

Whilst his fellow partygoers were engrossed in conversation with him and each other, Neil seemed not fully committed to what was now a debate and kept looking over his shoulder. Was he hoping she would come near or stay away? Was he looking out for her in hope or fear? His feelings were very mixed. He knew he was anxious but could not decide why. Perhaps it was a mixture of both hope and fear, all he knew was that he could feel his stomach sort of cringing every so often.

It was time to eat. Looking at the table plan that was pinned to the restaurant doors he just could not believe what he saw. The party planners had taken the list of staff and seated them together apparently in some order of seniority. This meant that Helen was seated right next to Neil and both, naturally along with other senior figures, near to Mr Crosby. Neil blinked and rubbed both his eyes half hoping he had misread the plan. No, he had not. There was the stark reality of what was about to happen. The meeting he had been avoiding all this time was now, within minutes, about to take place.

You may have heard the phrase 'going for a nervous pee' said of sportsmen before the game or job applicants before their interviews. If ever there was a time for a nervous pee it was now and off he went to find a toilet. Yes, it was partly a delaying tactic but he genuinely and suddenly felt very nervous with a great urge to pass water.

As he stood there in front of the urinals Neil decided to play it cool. He would put everything that went on in the past to the back of his mind. He would treat Helen almost like a stranger and not mention, or make any reference to, the relationship they had or the situation as it is now. After washing his hands he made his way back to the restaurant.

He greeted and acknowledged the boss and shook hands with the managers who he had not had the chance to meet when he arrived. Of course, he also shook hands with Helen although it all felt rather awkward. Neil, looking passed Helen at the boss, explained to those nearest to him, *"Sorry for being last, the call of nature you know."* He took his place at the table beside Helen.

Helen had a big grin on her face. Neither Neil nor Helen had anything to say certainly not to each other. Helen's grin broadened. Neil did not know what was amusing and looked towards her a little bewildered.

Helen then broke into a laugh and immediately smothered it with her napkin. Neil was really taken aback. Looked around the table to see who was pulling funny faces or doing something so hilarious to cause Helen's reaction. 'Nothing' he thought and he knew that no one had told a joke. Everyone had a happy smiling face, after all, it was a party, but he just could not see any reason for Helen's almost uncontrollable laughter. 'What could be so funny?' He wondered.

Just then Helen leaned over towards Neil put her arm around his shoulder and put her lips close to his right ear. 'Oh dear what's happening, I certainly did not expect this' his mind went into freefall. A shocked Neil just did not know what to do, where to put himself or what to say. So shocked he just froze like one of the hotel stone statues.

Helen whispered still with a stifled laugh "before you sat down I noticed your flies were open."

The statue came to life and immediately attended to the offending zip. Neil must have been so affected by the thoughts of the forthcoming meeting with Helen, and so on edge, that he neglected to 'adjust his dress.' I think that is the term used on some public notices of the time. 'Please adjust your dress[13] before leaving' - usually placed in a prominent position near the toilet exit.

Neil, with horror written all over his face, looked towards Helen. His eyes were popping out. Good job it was only his eyes. The skin around his face stretched and his lips clenched tight and thin with the horror and embarrassment of it all.

Helen looked towards Neil and she was still trying hard not to laugh. The look on his face was so funny it added to her need to laugh out loud. She just to say managed to stop another outburst of laughter from becoming full-blown.

He looked around the table hoping no one else had realised. It seemed they had not. He looked back at Helen saw that she was struggling to contain herself and within seconds Neil's sense of humour surfaced. His face relaxed into a smile and within a moment or two, both fell about laughing to the wonderment of their fellow diners.

"What's the big joke?" asked Ron. *"Aren't you going to share it with us?"*

"Oh! It's nothing Dad. Just one of those in-jokes that no one else would see the funny side of," returned Helen not wanting to embarrass Neil any more than he already had been.

He was very grateful for that. In a strange sort of way he was also very grateful he had left his trouser zip undone, albeit accidentally. The situation had been a great ice breaker between them and the rest of the meal continued with polite banter. Neither Neil nor Helen touched on any subject that would be liable to cause the return of the ice age.

At the end of the meal Mr Ronald Crosby, head of Crosby's Aluminium Foundry, stood up and made a speech. He was provided with a microphone for it was a large restaurant. He talked mainly about the factory and thanked everyone for what they had achieved in the past. He also talked about future plans. They would have to stop work for a few days but promised everyone would get paid to which a huge cheer went up. They would be halting production for a while but not because there was a lack of work. On the contrary, they were installing a new and faster set of presses and other equipment into the foundry. This would give them greater capacity. Towards the end of his speech, Ron made, what was to Neil, a devastating statement.

"I would now like to propose a toast to my beautiful daughter Helen. I am not going to go into detail because some things are better left unsaid, suffice to say she

has had a very difficult few years. I want everyone to know that I am very proud of her and I am going to be very sad when she leaves to make a new life for herself in Australia."

'WHAT?' shouted Neil inside his head which seemed almost audible. He visibly jolted in his chair when he heard that. A huge bolt of lightning had just struck him in the ribs, followed by a deep sense of desolation.

Mr Crosby continued, *"I will miss her very much and hope to travel to see her…"* stumbling with his words a little at this point, *"….well…as often as possible. She has made this decision for herself and I do understand why. Pat, one of her old university friend's living in Perth, Western Australia, said they would be very pleased to look after her until she finds a job and somewhere to live."*

"So I give you a toast; to Helen and her new life down under."

Everyone stood, and enthusiastically echoed the toast, *"To Helen."*

I said everyone but there was one person who was not at all enthusiastic. Neil, eventually rose slowly but only because he felt the unspoken insistence of the crowd forcing him to his feet. In what could only be called 'just about' a standing position reluctantly he raised his glass and said quietly, almost after everyone else had finished, *"To Helen."* Then sat back down with a face so very forlorn.

Now he was really confused. Why should he feel such emotion and a distinct dislike of the prospect of never seeing Helen again? After all, had he not made up his mind that he could never be in love with the woman who killed his wife? Neil seemed to be in a daydream. His eyes stared and everyone else seemed to be invisible and inaudible to him. The parting words he used to Helen, once more filled his mind 'I wish you well…   …have a good life. I just know…   …some lucky man… …whose life …   …made complete when he finds you, but for us this is goodbye…'

'…for us this is goodbye.'

'...for us this is goodbye.'

This, it seemed, indeed, was goodbye forever to Neil's chance of love.

He suddenly, jolted from his dream-like state by the band striking up, got up, made his excuses and left the table. If it wasn't for a taxi pre-booked for a certain time Neil would have left the hotel there and then. He was certainly in no mood to party but did not want to spoil anyone else's enjoyment.

For the rest of the evening, Neil went back to the 'avoiding Helen' strategy he used before they were both plunged together at the dining table. He not only avoided Helen he avoided everyone. He loosened his bow tie and collar then sat by himself drowning his sorrows at a remote table in one of the bars away from the ballroom. As the evening grew late, he went to say goodnight to the boss. It was probably about ten minutes before the taxi was due.

"Where have you been all evening, I haven't seen you since dinner?" Ron inquired.

"No, well, err, I haven't been feeling too good," came Neil's reply which was certainly not a lie. If anything it was an understatement.

Knowing exactly what was wrong with Neil, Ron apologised. *"Look I know that was a shock for a lot of people and I know it was for you as well but I promised Helen not to tell anyone until everything was organised and when the time was right. Of course, I don't want her to go but I can understand the way she is thinking and I must support her. It would be selfish of me not to."*

Neil nodded in agreement and Ron continued, *"I said I would never get involved in Helen's love life. I am going to break that promise now by telling you that she still loves you. That is why she is going away. She is desperately trying to mend her life and it is heartbreaking for me and her to know that she will not be able to mend it here with you the person she loves. That does not mean I am attaching any blame to you. I understand and respect your point of view. There I have broken my promise."*

Not really knowing what to say, Neil just excused himself as his taxi would be waiting outside.

"Well I had better get back to my guests, anyway," said Ron.

As he walked away Neil turned back towards Ron and asked, *"When does she go?"*

"End of March," Ron answered.

"Taxi for Mr Collins" A shout was heard from the foyer and Neil went out not having to and not really wanting to face Helen.

CHAPTER TEN:
An Encounter of the Altogether Different Kind.

Thanks to Jenny and her family, Neil enjoyed some Christmas celebrations and had a night out with his old friend Dave. However, Christmas 1965 still proved to be one of the loneliest he had experienced.

It was now a few days into the beginning of the New Year. Neil pondered as to what 1966 would bring. He knew it was a big year for Crosby's with all the planned changes and expansion and once again he threw himself into his work. Yet every private moment seemed to be taken up wrestling. Wrestling with his emotions like, had he done right by Helen? Had she done right by him? He had been told she still loved him. 'If that is true why would she go away?' he asked himself, and answered, realising it could have something to do with having made it quite clear he could not love her, and that they were finished for good, although this was far from clear to him.

Neil arrived home, on the evening of Wednesday 12th January 1966, very tired. He had been in charge of installing new presses, to replace and almost double the number of old ones. As this meant the factory virtually closing down for a few days he had to work hard to get it finished within a short time scale. He had worked all weekend also Monday and Tuesday from early morning to late at night. He started work today at 6.00a.m. and had just got in as his clock chimed 8.00p.m.

He had finished the work to reorganise the foundry and install all the new equipment. All that was left to do tomorrow was a test run before they would be back to full production. In fact better than full production because the newly equipped foundry had speeded things up and improved capacity by more than 50% allowing the company to accept more orders and become much more profitable. Neil was in for a promotion, a salary increase and a large bonus on top. 'It will all have been worth it.'

Not having the energy to start cooking he decided to settle down on the couch to read the paper, eat a pie and drink a bottle of his favourite brown ale. He usually ate well and knew it was important to nourish his body as well as exercise it but, on this one occasion, he just could not be bothered to stand for half an hour or more in the kitchen.

Yes, he had thrown himself into his work, after all, what else was there left for him? He looked up from his paper to the sideboard where his photographs were displayed and pondered his future. Would he ever find love again? He looked across at Fiona and Helen's photographs. He wasn't actively looking for love he never had been since he lost Fiona. If Helen had not sought him out, he would not have fallen for her.

He was conscious that he had become quite lonely. It was more evident when he was off work. It would hit him hard when he had time to think like now. He looked around the room as if to acknowledge its emptiness. Not of furniture or photographs, there were plenty of those, but of another human being to share his life with. He scanned the scene as if on a panoramic camera, pausing momentarily when his eyes again met Fiona's photograph and then similarly at Helen's photograph which he had purposely left on display despite everything.

Of course, he often thought about Fiona, his first love, but was able now to keep the tears in check and smile at the funny things she had said and the happy times they spent together. To a great extent he had tried to stop feeling sorry for himself but at the same time knew that apart from his work, especially now there was no Helen, his life, in general, was not what he would have hoped for. Neil discovered that loneliness can't always be overcome by being with lots of other people. He had tried going to friend's parties or events where there were other people but he got this feeling of loneliness even in a crowded room. There was a big hole in his life that was left by Fiona's death. It was a large hole that he thought could never be filled. He did, for a short while, feel that this chasm would be healed, if only partly, by Helen.

Helen appeared to be OK with that and the fact that no one could take Fiona's place in Neil's life was understandable. From Neil's history shared with Helen of his love for Fiona and vice versa, she could see that Fiona was special and never tried to take her place. She did, of course, cling on to the hope that one day, it may take a long time, but that one day, he would feel the same way about her. But that was not a priority for Helen. Right there and then all she wanted was to love him and be loved in return, now of course that will never be.

"Neil," a voice whispered. *"Neil,"* it came again a little louder this time. He looked towards the part of his room from where the voice emanated, *"Neil my love."*

He recognised that sweet voice but could not believe his eyes. It was Fiona. This could not be - he must be seeing things. He shook his head and smacked his face and still he could see her. It wasn't the drink he had only had the one bottle.

"Fiona!" he shouted as he jumped up and made his way towards her flinging his arms open for a long-awaited embrace. He was jolted to a halt by her unexpected reply and reaction to his naturally enthusiastic welcome. She put both arms straight out in front with the palms of her hands facing him.

"No, don't come any closer," she insisted. *"I can't stay long. The laws do not allow me to be here but I just had to visit you."*

"But please!" He implored her as he advanced a little nearer and was again repelled.

"No Neil," this was a command. He realised she meant business. *"Please sit back down.* She appeared to take a breath. *"I have a message for you my darling,"* she said very softly and lovingly.

Neil, although reluctantly, did as Fiona had ordered him to do. *"A message?"* he repeated in a mumble, now very bewildered by it all.

Fiona picked up the photograph of Helen from the sideboard and moved closer to Neil *"Please do not try to touch me,"* she affirmed as she drew closer. *"I have come to set you free."*

Neil spoke. *"But,"* trying to ask her, set me free from what?

Fiona put her finger on his lips. *"Hush,"* she said then sat beside him. *"I cannot stay long, please just listen."*

Neil was of course surprised by all this but even more surprised when he could not feel the touch of her finger on his lips. A shiver ran down his spine and his hair stood on end but he still found himself nodding obediently in agreement to her request to sit still and listen.

"You have been faced with a dilemma, and I want you to know I am very proud of you. I want you to know that where I am all we ever want for those we leave behind is happiness." Holding up and pointing to the photograph of Helen she continued. *"Helen is a good person and she loves you very dearly. I am happy for you to be with her, despite the outcome of the accident and I set you free to do so. You and I will always love each other, that will never change, but you must not let your love for me prevent you from gaining the happiness I know could be yours."*

Fiona paused and then as if she decided Neil needed more convincing added.

"I have spoken to Barry, Helen's son and he too would be delighted for both of you to get together. I have got to go now. I have stayed too long." With that she placed

the photograph of Helen on the coffee table walked towards the window, turned, blew Neil a kiss then vanished.

Neil was at first unable to move. Something, he did not know what, kept him glued to the couch. All he could do was lift his arms to beckon her back and call her name. Suddenly the force field holding him down gave way just at the same time as he used all his strength to try once more to get up and follow her. He fell very hard on the floor and woke up!

"Oh no, not another dream!" he cried out loud as he remained still for a moment realising he had hurt himself. 'Nothing serious' he thought as he struggled to get back on to the couch where he had obviously fallen asleep the night before just as he did on a previous occasion. He was a little bit bruised both physically and mentally. It is quite a shock to hit the floor at any time but to be woken up by it is not good for the system. Of course, when he woke up he momentarily did not have a clue where he was or what he was doing. The dream suddenly came back to him. It did not seem dream-like at the time, but what other explanation could there be?

He sat for quite some time mulling over the experience. He realised the significance of it. Fiona had come to him and made it quite clear that she was more than happy for him to love Helen and share their lives together. 'She has set me free from my dilemma.'

He brought to mind that in the cafe he had believed Helen's reasoning and regrets and forgave her for everything. He had finished with her because, and only because, she was the cause of Fiona's death. Had she been the same person but without that history, he would still be with her. But Fiona's visit and message had set him free and there were now no barriers. This lifted his spirits and made him feel quite light-hearted. Then his mood changed when he gave more thought to what had happened.

'Yeh!' he thought in a dismissive manner, 'but it was just a dream. It was something out of my own head. I cannot give it any credence. I once dreamt I could fly without an aeroplane. Just me on my own, not even any wings. I did not even have to flap my arms I could just fly. So how can I give credence or meaning to any dream?'

He sat there on the couch for quite a while thinking, arguing with himself and rubbing his arm, elbow and shoulder that took the main impact of his fall.

He looked across to the clock 'I think I need some coffee. It is getting late.' As he did this he also glanced at Fiona's photograph and he was immediately aware that Helen's photograph was not on the sideboard where it normally is. The shivers that he experienced in his dream once again ran down his spine when he realised that now her picture was **there**....on the coffee table where Fiona had placed it before she made her mysterious exit. **'This cannot be'** he confirmed and questioned his own sanity. 'Am I still dreaming?' he thought as the hairs on the back of his neck stood up for the second time in what seemed like just minutes. He realised that Helen's picture had apparently moved from one place to another..... By itself!?

He knew he hadn't moved it and last night **was** just a dream.... wasn't it?

[A few days later]

Neil, after giving it a great deal of thought eventually believed that whether the encounter with Fiona was a real spiritual visitation or just a very special dream he should regard it as a clear green light to building a future for himself with Helen. Without the mysterious movement of the photograph, he may have dismissed it as just a fanciful dream. He was now very sure of what to do next.

He had not dashed out to see her or rushed to the telephone. This was not an overnight decision; he took several days of careful consideration over it. Now he was absolutely resolute; he would contact Helen and meet up for a chat, after all, there was now only a few weeks left to stop her from travelling.

He ordered a large bouquet of flowers and had them sent to her address. The card read…

'Would you meet me for coffee on Saturday at ten o'clock? Our usual cafe. X'

She still had not replied by the Thursday of that week. It was Ron who said to him at work that day. *"Helen asked me to pass a message on to you. She will meet you as suggested. I meant to tell you the day before yesterday but things got a bit hectic."*

Neil gave a sigh of relief.

"Phew! Thanks. Please tell her I'm looking forward to it."

Helen was very surprised, to say the least at receiving such a lovely bouquet. She was also very surprised at the invitation to meet up although she had always planned to say a proper goodbye to him. 'Perhaps he had just pre-empted that and wanted to say a proper farewell himself,' she decided, but thought 'It's a little bit early for goodbyes I'm not due to set off to stay with my friend Jill, in London, till the 21st March.'

[Saturday 22nd January 1966 in the cafe]

They turned up almost simultaneously and when they walked through the door. Luigi grimaced and murmured in a sort of quiet splutter.

"Oh-a no! not-a you again?" but before they could notice, his less than friendly demeanour was soon replaced by his customer friendly face. He remembered they were going to spend some money.

Neil so wanted to hug her, just take her into his arms and squeeze, but he realised that would be too full on when she did not even know why he had asked to meet her. They exchanged the usual pleasantries. Neil purchased their coffees and they sat down.

"*So, this is our final goodbye then,*" said Helen still thinking it was a little premature. Before Neil had a chance to reply she continued, "*Thank you for the flowers, they were really beautiful, it was such a nice parting gift. You were always very thoughtful and romantic.*" Just for a second, she focused her gaze into his eyes wishing things could have been different. "*I had every intention of seeing you before I set off for Australia. I would never have gone without saying a final goodbye.*"

All this talk about goodbyes and final and parting was not the way Neil had envisaged their meeting. He was forced into an immediate impulsive reply, "*But that's just it, I haven't come here to say goodbye to you, Helen. I love you and I want you to stay.*"

Helen was absolutely flabbergasted. In fact, to say she was flabbergasted is a complete understatement. She certainly was not expecting to hear that and could not form the words in her head to reply. If she had the mouth would not have functioned well enough to say them. All that came out was, "*A, err, no, em, what?*" and her ramblings were interrupted and the interruption would cause her flabber to become even more gasted because she certainly wasn't expecting what came next.

'Now!' thought Neil. 'Do it now!' His early impulsiveness now gave way to what he had been planning. Getting down on one knee, Neil pulled from his pocket a box. He opened it to reveal a very beautiful diamond encrusted engagement ring and got straight to the point.

"*Will you please marry me?*" as he offered up the ring.

The customers were suddenly interested in what was going on and Luigi once again hearing a disruption found himself saying, out of the corner of his mouth.

"*What-a the hell's-a going on now?*"

You would think that there could only be one of two possible answers to Neil's plea to Helen, yes or no. How wrong can we be? Having stared at Neil and the ring for a few seconds she finally delivered her answer. She bent down towards him so that only he could hear.

"Get up and get back on your seat, now!" she said vehemently through gritted teeth. *"Everyone is looking at us."*

He did so and put the ring on the table, back in its box, but symbolically with the lid open and facing towards Helen, so as to keep her options open. After a few seconds of sharing an uncomfortable silence, Neil ventured. *"Do I take that as a no, then?"*

"Yes, you do!" She quickly and angrily retorted. Then continued a tirade, *"Last time we sat here you had been hurting because of what I had done to you. Since then I have been hurting every day. Do you really think after all I have gone through and after all the difficult decisions I have had to make about leaving my father? After all the planning and organising I have done for my long sea trip. Letters I have written documents I have had to gather along with all the forms I have had to complete. Do you really think, after all that, I can change my mind,"* clicking her fingers and almost taking Neil's nose off, ***"just like that?"*** *I have been through huge emotional turmoil culminating in a final decision to say goodbye to my father, to my home, to my friends and to you. Even though, I love you so much."* She quickly corrected herself, *"Emm, I **loved** you so much."* She paused for the correction to sink in. *"After all this, do you think, at the drop of a hat, I can just put everything into reverse?* **No, NO!"** As she raised her voice she banged her fist on the table.

"Everything all-a right-a?" Luigi thought he had better check for the health and safety of his customers and his crockery. Neil and Helen with sullen faces just turned to him smiled, nodded and turned back to each other resuming their original long faces. Helen's angry and long, Neil's sad and long.

"I have gone right off my coffee now I think it would be best if I go," decided Helen as she started to get up from the table.

Neil grabbed her wrist, *"Don't, please don't go,"* as he said this he let her go remembering the last time he had grasped her wrist tightly. They both thought the same but neither mentioned it. *"Please, I once gave you the time and space to explain things to me. Please hear me out. You at least owe me that."*

Yes, she did owe him that and she duly sat down and began again drinking her coffee. Neil carefully explained to Helen his dilemma about loving someone who was responsible for the death of his wife. Whilst he had forgiven Helen, and he knew Fiona wanted him to live his life to the full with someone new, he did not believe that it could or should be with the one who killed her. He felt that would be a betrayal and a step too far.

She understood that and now for the first time had an intimate insight into his thinking and could exactly pinpoint what it was that had finally come between them. Neil went on to explain his dream or spiritual encounter that he believed changed everything. He had been visited by Fiona; somehow he wasn't sure how. All he knew was that there was physical evidence of her visit after she had gone. He explained all that to Helen. The photograph had definitely moved from, its original position on the sideboard, to the coffee table.

He told her that the reason he had been visited was, using Fiona's very words, *"I have come to set you free."* He continued, *"I am convinced that I am now free to be with you. I have never stopped loving you I have just suppressed my love for you because of my loyalty to and love for Fiona,"* Neil explained. He pleaded, *"Can't you see what that means? There is nothing stopping us now, and a little dickey-bird did tell me you still love me."* He was referring of course to her father. *"I love you and I want to marry you."*

They had finished their coffees and finished just about all that was to be said but Neil did not get the response he was hoping and praying for.

Feeling very emotional Helen stood up and looked down at Neil. Closing the lid over the ring in front of her she pushed the box back towards him, as a physical demonstration of her final answer. She then started to speak, her voice breaking up...

"I wish you well and hope you have a good life. I just know there is some lucky woman out there whose life will be made complete when she finds you, but for us this is goodbye."

Now sobbing her heart out Helen left the cafe and Neil for the last time. She did not mean to have a dig at him by using the words that Neil had once spoken to her. You could see by the emotional mess she was in that the use of those same words wasn't meant to hurt him. It was meant from someone who felt weak and vulnerable inside, as a strong outward sign of a final, no turning back, message of goodbye. She did not look back and ran out of the cafe into the street.

Some of the customers were now looking to the owner for answers. Luigi looked back at them shrugged his shoulders with upturned hands and made that 'do not-a ask-a me' facial expression then went back to his work.

Neil sat there feeling very lonely. He was lonelier now than ever before. He cursed himself for not having acted more quickly and/or for not acting differently when there was still time. He sat there for a long time thinking and sipping on a now empty cup. Several thoughts were going through his mind 'what's the use, there is nothing left for me now, my life is finished,' and other negatives of a similar nature.

Before going home he called into St Mary's Church and kneeled in one of the pews to pray quietly to himself.

'Lord Jesus my friend you know everything about me. You know why I felt the need to come here today. I ask for your help. I love you Lord, please help me, please help me...

So sad is my heart...

Lord please, help me.'

Amen.

CHAPTER ELEVEN: The Acceptance.

A few days later we find Neil in deep distress. He was very cross with himself for allowing his love to escape. Some of his friends, for example, at the local pub tried to help. They tried to cheer him up. You know the old sayings people rely on at times like that.... *"There's plenty more fish in the sea."* Of course, that really did not help at all.

For quite some time now Neil had not been himself. He tried to keep working but just seemed to be going downhill rapidly. Among other things, he needed to rest. He had been working very hard over many weeks. That and all the emotional turmoil had taken it out of him. He tried to pull himself around but after a few days, he still had not come to terms with the situation, in fact, things were getting worse. He started smoking cigarettes, almost to chain smoking standard. He wasn't sleeping very well, he felt physically ill, and he had no desire to go out anywhere. He cringed at the thought of a morning run that he used to enjoy so much. He felt as if his life was a mess. He began to think that the outcome of most of the events praying on his mind may all be his fault.

He reported into work sick over the telephone and apologised to his boss. *"Ron I am really sorry but I cannot come to work. I do not fully understand what is wrong with me but I know I am not well. If I try to keep going and come to work, I may end up having an accident with one of the presses and causing myself or someone else an injury."*

Ron knew Neil quite well by this time and he realised he was normally a very positive kind of guy. He accepted that he certainly did not sound his old self and said, *"You will be going to the doctors then?"* with a slight hint of 'that's an order' in his voice.

"OK! - Yes, yes sure," came Neil's, not very enthusiastic reply.

"Anyway just get yourself better and pulled around as soon as you can, for your own sake," said Ron and added, *"but I must admit things won't run quite as smoothly without you here Neil."*

"OK! - I will get back soon. Bye," said Neil but did not even convince himself.

A normally clean and tidy flat was starting to look like a jumble sale that a bomb had just exploded in. Old newspapers, empty beer bottles, half-eaten take-ways and discarded clothes littered the sofa and floor. Almost every surface had something cluttering it up. The surfaces that were free of clutter were covered in thick dust. He had not vacuumed for many a day but in a perverse sort of way that did not matter because you couldn't see the detritus left on the carpet for the other jumble left strewn around.

Not normally a smoker his saucers and old tin lids became full of ash and old cigarette stubs. No clothes washing had been done, there were no clean towels left in the cupboard and Neil was still using the same drying up towel over and over again until it had started to turn brown. His answer to that – he stopped washing up! He stopped washing himself and the crockery, leaving the dirty cups to mount up, one on top of the other like the leaning tower of Pisa. Good job, or bad job, depending on how you look at it, that he had a plentiful supply. When the supply did run out he just kept giving the last cup a quick rinse. He soon stopped drinking tea anyway and just drank straight from the beer bottle. He snacked on crisps and other rubbish. He had not shaved for days, so with his scruffy beard and matted hair, he looked a sight. He was a wreck and fast becoming a nervous wreck. He started shaking until he had another beer. Sometimes shaking with sorrow for himself and probably shaking with lack of nourishment. His thoughts ran wild as he became even more convinced that he was to blame for everything.

He was in the depths of despair. He had never been so low even when he lost Fiona, probably because there were plenty of people around him at that time. He pulled through and though he had got pretty low it was never like this. Of course not only was he still trying to cope with losses in the past he was now faced with even more loss.

There was only one thing in a worse mess than his flat and that was his mental state.

[Friday 18th February 1966]

Neil's best mate was in town and decided to look him up. 'He may fancy a pint' thought Dave as he knocked on the door. He knocked again. He could hear the TV so 'He must be at home' Dave thought and knocked even louder. After what seemed to be an age Neil's dishevelled silhouette appeared from behind the partly opened door.

Dave knew immediately there was something wrong. He had never seen Neil look or to be blunt, smell like he did. Even when he was in his mechanics overalls having just spent hours laying under the chassis of an oil and mud splattered car he looked better than he did today.

*"What on **earth** is the matter?"* said a very shocked Dave.

"I am just not well at the moment," said Neil falteringly and asked, *"Do... do you want to come in?"* hoping Dave would say no.

Dave did go in, if rather reluctantly, as he had caught a glimpse of the carnage as Neil moved to one side and the smell got worse as he entered. Needless to say, he did not ask him out for a drink and he did not stay long.

"You will have to excuse the mess I have not tidied up today yet," Neil explained.

If the situation was not so serious this statement would have normally played directly to Dave's sense of humour and he would by now, be in fits of laughter. He knew it was no joke and after trying to get to the bottom of the problem and not really hearing anything that made much sense, he wished him all the best and left.

Luckily for Neil, Dave did prove to be a good friend. When he returned home he immediately called Neil's sister Jenny and explained what he had found. He told her what the flat and Neil looked like. She was very shocked and in some ways knew it was so unlike Neil that Dave must be exaggerating at least a little bit. He wasn't. However, as Dave did not normally contact her and she could tell by his voice this was not one of his jokes, she agreed to come to Scarborough the very next day to see for herself.

"I called you because I want to help. He certainly needs help and I just know you are the one that can sort him out," concluded Dave as they ended their conversation. Once Dave was off the phone Jenny phoned Neil. Naturally, she was very concerned and told him she would come and see him tomorrow, first thing.

The next day Jenny was true to her word and arrived early in the morning. Again there was a reluctance to come to the door and again, the dishevelled appearance but this time, a different reception for his visitor. Neil almost fell into her arms crying profusely as they stood on the doorstep. Loud sobs and convulsive shakes of emotion interspersed every word. *"I....am....so...so....pleased....to....see....you,"* he managed to say, holding on to her very tightly. He was almost collapsing with emotion and Jenny helped him back into the room, pushing the debris out of the way, sat him and herself down on the sofa. She hugged him until he had regained some composure.

"I wish you had called me sooner. Tell me, what is the matter?"

"It's all my fault," Neil said quietly but then emphasised, "It's... **all... my... fault!**" and began to cry once more, wailing very loudly, now that he felt able to let it all out.

After a very short time, Jenny realised this was something she could not deal with by herself. Things had gone so far that Neil needed professional help. She could do the cleaning and she did. It did not take long for the flat to be gleaming once more and smelling sweet. She was quite able to look after Neil but she just knew his mental state was not something that could be left to chance. 'Time alone will not put this right, he needed medical help and he needed it fast,' she thought.

Jenny insisted he visited the doctor. *"Can you visit him or shall I call him out?"* she asked. By now even Neil realised it was the only option so Jenny didn't need to insist that much.

Neil answered, *"I will go and see him, but will you phone the surgery, I'm in no condition to face those frosty faced receptionists even on the phone.*[14]*"*

"Ok," she said *"I will sort it."*

Jenny rang the doctor's surgery and made the appointment.

"I am afraid the first appointment we have available is a week on Thursday," said the surly receptionist. Neil, listening in, had had dealings with her before. Remembering when he first went to register with them, Neil thought, 'the receptionists are like minders doing their best to keep the patients away from the doctors, it's like dealing with the Gestapo' *"Is there really nothing sooner?"* Jenny asked bravely.

"No, I am sorry, that is all we have at 2 o'clock with Dr Brown."

"I will take it then," said Jenny.

Neil chimed in *"I could be dead by then,"* not realising the receptionist could hear him. She quickly replied, *"Well if that was to happen be sure to call and cancel the appointment,"* and put the phone down.

Feeling very vulnerable Neil just accepted the date, shook his head at the receptionist's manner, sat back down and said to Jenny sarcastically, *"That is exactly what I needed, a kind friendly caring helpful voice, on the other end of the phone. I hope the doctor is a little more sympathetic."*

'No wonder Neil did not want to make the phone call,' thought Jenny as she picked the receiver back up. She was not happy at all and was just about to ring back, *"I will give that bitch a piece of my mind."*

"No, don't "Implored Neil, "they are always like that and it won't do any good."

Neil spent those long days waiting for his appointment not knowing what to do with himself. He didn't go out but he didn't want to stay in. He went to bed but could not sleep. He didn't want to stay in bed in the mornings yet felt he had nothing to get up for. He cried a lot, smoked a lot and felt very sorry for himself. He picked at his food and only tried hard to eat because of Jenny's encouragement and the fact that she had made some of his meals especially for him. She could not stay all the time but she had managed to bring him back from the brink with long sympathetic chats. At the same time offering practical help and reasoned advice which usually Neil would have already sussed for himself. This and the fact that he knew Jenny would be back soon kept him on the straight and narrow. She promised to come with him to the doctors mainly because she thought it best if he didn't drive while he was so depressed.

Not only was the house clean now but so was Neil. The Thursday of his appointment came and Neil had managed to smarten himself up even more. He made a special effort to look presentable to the doctor. Thankfully and with the help of Jenny's gentle but firm encouragement he still had a bit of sense left in his mixed up brain to force his body to get its act together and present itself sober and clean at the surgery. They arrived fifteen minutes before the allotted time.

He sat nervously reading the notices on the wall. He then turned his attention to the magazines purposely left out for patients to read during their inevitable long wait as delays often happened - and Neil had arrived **early?**

Flicking through them, wondering if he will find any up to date news, having not read a paper for weeks, he chose what appeared to be the newest magazine in the pile. It was certainly not the latest issue but it seemed to be the least dog-eared, the less torn and dirty out of the bunch, containing what he hoped was fairly recent news in comparison to the rest.

As Jenny was checking her diary, he read one of the reports with great interest before replacing the magazine back on the table. He turned to Jenny and said, *"I have just read the breaking news, isn't it a shame?"* Her mouth turned down at the edges and her eyes narrowed and looked down her nose as if to say 'I don't know what you mean' and he delivered the punch line, *"About the Titanic!"* with a slight smile on his lips. She chuckled and felt a certain ease. This was the first time since she rescued him that his sense of humour became apparent once more.

He was just about to start on the children's comics when he was called in to see the doctor. Naturally, Jenny stayed in the waiting room. She had already given Neil his orders to tell the doctor everything.

Following the normal pleasantries, Neil started to explain how he felt.

"I can be emotional," explained Neil to Doctor Brown, *"that's normal for me, now and then, but nowadays I just seem to cry over anything. I can be just sitting watching television or reading the paper and without any rhyme or reason, I just burst into tears. Even **I** know that is just not right for anyone and certainly not for me."* Within a minute or two of meeting Dr Brown, Neil sensed that he was friendly and most importantly approachable.

So Neil continued, *"I am tired all the time yet I am not sleeping as well as I used to."*

Dr Brown spent quite some time with Neil. He had only seen him once since he first registered so knew he was not the sort of patient that would make an appointment on a whim.

Neil spilt his heart and soul out and Dr Brown listened very carefully and sympathetically. *"I have not had the easiest of lives Doctor. When I was very young both my parents died within months of each other. My Aunty Annie, who cared for both me and my sister, also died when I was a teenager. As an adult, I have lost my first love, Fiona. She died in a car accident and I was driving at the time. I also came close to death in that accident and I am beginning to wonder that it may have been better if I had died.*

In recent years I have suffered a series of lies and deceit perpetrated by Helen the second love of my life. I thought I could trust her and she betrayed that trust. It is too complicated to go into detail about now, but it did hurt."

Dr Brown nodded.

*"I still love her despite the betrayal. I thought she loved me. I even asked her to marry me but I have been rejected. Now she has left me; I will never see her again. She is immigrating to Australia. So I have lost the two people who meant the most to me in my adult years and I just cannot cope. In fact, I mean, Dr Brown, I **really** cannot cope with it anymore."*
"All right Neil." The Dr, Brown tried to calm him seeing he was very affected by his own story. Then to try and reassure him, he continued, *"I am sure I can help you but first is there anything more you feel you want to tell me?"*

He did not tell the doctor about the state he allowed himself and the house to get into, he was too ashamed of that but continued...

*"Perhaps the worst thing of all, right at this minute, I really believe that all of it is my fault. Had I turned the steering wheel the other way just before the collision, perhaps I would be dead and Fiona may have lived. I have no recollection of the accident or indeed what action I took if any, but it still haunts me when I question my reactions that day. Then there is my procrastination about making a commitment to Helen. I have stifled any chance of winning back the love Helen had for me and now it's too late. Too late and it's **entirely my fault.**"* Neil began to weep openly but managed to pull himself around not wanting to appear a complete wimp in front of his doctor.

"Please excuse me, Doctor, because, up to a few weeks ago, I had been working very hard doing lots of overtime and things just seem to be getting me down. I still feel very tired and depressed and I think you are my last resort." Neil offered this as a reason for his emotion and his visit. *"I am falling to pieces doctor, I know I am. I am no longer able to go to work, I am drinking too much and I am not eating properly. I am not taking care of myself I have even started smoking."*

"Well at least what you have just said is a very good sign," announced Doctor Brown. Neil looked at him questioningly without speaking and the doctor picked that up. *"Ah! Well, you see most people who come in here will not admit their failings and certainly never admit to drinking too much."* This brought a smile to Neil's face.

Dr Brown delivered his diagnosis. *"You're obviously suffering from a mixture of depression and fatigue. I will give you a month's supply of these."* He scribbled on his prescription pad, tore off the top copy and handed it to Neil. *"They are Barbiturates[15]; you need to take two each day in the evening. They are called phenobarbitone and they are very strong. Do not,* **under any circumstances,** *take more than the stated dose."* The doctor thought for a moment and gave Neil time to assimilate his previous instructions. Then continued...

"I want you to rest. That is, stay off work but get some light relaxing exercise. Take things easy but at the same time keep yourself, especially your mind, busy. Take a nice walk, often and get plenty of fresh air, that sort of thing. Take up a hobby. Do things to take your mind off your problems. Try not to be alone for long periods. Visit some friends who are not likely to rake over the coals."

Neil could see the sense in what the doctor was saying and nodded in agreement.

"I want you to come back in three weeks when the tablets I have given you are nearly finished and we can talk again. These tablets are just a temporary aid; I will not be giving you anymore because they can become addictive. If when you see me again you feel no better I will arrange an appointment for some counselling sessions with a psychoanalyst."

The doctor believed this was serious. He handed Neil another piece of paper. It was a sort of brochure.

"If you start to feel any worse or have any thoughts about committing suicide, ring my surgery and I will see you as an emergency patient at a moment's notice."

Neil gave the doctor an odd concerned look and thought 'what about the Gestapo?'

As if to be able to read Neil's mind Dr Brown said: *"Don't worry I will leave specific instructions for my staff on the reception desk."* Neil gave an audible sigh of relief.
"I have also given you the telephone number and information about an organisation called the Samaritans. I do not think you are at that point at the moment and I hope you would never get anywhere near contemplating ending your life, but please, promise me you will ring them and me if ever you feel so low."

Quite a contradiction really – Barbiturates and advice about the Samaritans. At least he was not going to keep the tablets going, long term. This must have been some sort of divine foresight for Dr Brown and divine intervention for Neil.
The doctor ended their session by saying, *"These tablets will help to relax you and take a little bit of the weight off your shoulders. They will also help you to sleep but you really must help yourself as well. Cut out your drinking completely while you're on the tablets because they will react adversely to alcohol. Don't operate any machinery and if you need to drive do it in the mornings providing you're not feeling tired or dizzy."* He paused then said finally placing a friendly hand on his shoulder, *"Finally, start eating correctly. If ever your body needed good nourishment it is now.... and after all... you're worth it."*

Neil could feel the sadness welling up again that had made him so emotional earlier. How kind and thoughtful the doctor had been. Having felt pretty worthless for some time the doctor's words of reassurance were just what he needed to hear. Fighting to stay in control he made his exit as quickly as it was possible without being rude. The doctor had not minced words but that was probably just what he needed. The doctor was also aware that a lot of the problems were in Neil's mind and he had purposely given him a lift, with those encouraging words, before he left the surgery.

Shocked by the doctor's diagnosis Neil thought, 'am I really that close to wishing for death?' as he made his way to the chemists with Jenny and never mentioned that bit to her. He was though buoyed by the doctor's words of encouragement he promised himself he would carry out the doctor's instructions to the letter.

He did share all the information, apart from the suicidal bit, with Jenny and hid the leaflet about the Samaritans in his pocket before leaving the doctor's surgery.

He duly took the tablets as had been prescribed. These did seem to help a little and within a few days, he was out again on long walks. He kept himself busy as the doctor had suggested. He took the opportunity to visit Jenny and a few long lost friends whom he had not seen for a while including Dave and thanked him for getting in touch with Jenny. He also gave him the bad news; he would not be drinking for quite some time.

Neil joined the local library and started to read. He was mostly interested in true stories. Books like those about history or human achievement. Autobiographies and biographies were good as long as they were about important people. He wasn't at all interested in most of the so-called celebrities.

[21st March 1966]

The physical rest, the tablets and his faith began to heal him. He realised very well that God did not always give the answers to prayers in the way one would like. He also knew that Christians were to cherish their lives and not try to end them, before their natural term is up, no matter what the situation. One of the things that he thinks actually shocked him into recovery was Doctor Brown's diagnosis. 'He actually thought I may get close to killing myself.' Neil shuddered as he came across the brochure about the Samaritans. 'I will not need that now' he said to himself yet filed it safely in a draw, rather than throwing it away.

As he had not heard anything to the contrary he assumed Helen had now set off on her long trip to Australia. She was due to leave today the 21st, spending a few days with an old college friend, 'Jill I think they call her,' he pondered, 'living in London who she hadn't seen for a long time.' A few days later she would then travel to Southampton to board the liner 'Fairsea' setting sail for Freemantle on the 27th. Her Australian friend, Pat, would pick her up and take her to her temporary home in Perth.

Neil had come to accept things as they were. It took time and the intervention of Dave, Jenny and the doctor. 'God works in mysterious ways' he mused and took out a copy of a prayer he once was given. It had helped him on a previous occasion, called the serenity prayer. He rediscovered it in the back of his bible and read it out loud...

"God grant me the serenity to accept the things I cannot change, the courage to change the things I can and the wisdom to know the difference."

[The next day]

His boss had often phoned to ask how he was and whilst he was anxious to get him back to work he was genuinely interested in Neil's wellbeing and often offered to help with anything that he needed help with.

This time it was Neil's turn to make the phone call.
"I am feeling a lot better now," he reported to Ron. *"I have to see the doctor again in two days' time but I am sure I will be back to work a week on Monday."*

"That is really good news, Neil, I am so pleased to hear that you are well again."

A few words were exchanged about the latest happenings on the foundry floor and just before he rang off Ron said, *"Helen said to wish you well."* There was a silence, almost as if the line had gone dead. *"Hello... Neil... Are you still there?"*

Finally, Neil replied, *"She **has** gone then?"*

"Well, yes," as if there could be any other outcome. Of course, she had gone what did he expect? Ron continued, *"I am really sorry things did not*

work out between you. As I have already explained I didn't want her to go. That was mostly for my own selfish reasons. However, I have also grown very fond of you. You are a good man. I have been quietly working behind the scenes on, I assumed, behalf of you both. If things had worked out between you that would not only have given my daughter a good reason to stay but I would have gained a son-in-law and hopefully several grandchildren. After all, I am not getting any younger."

They both had a little chuckle at that. Then Ron resumed his explanation of the situation as he saw it.

"I am aware that I kept saying I was not going to get involved in her love life but I regularly broke that promise to myself. I urged her to tell you the truth about her past sooner. I often put a good word in for you when I spoke to her. I would have been very happy if you two had got together. It was me who changed the hotel restaurant seating plan at the party to make sure you were sitting side by side. Even at that late stage when all the plans were made and she had her travel documents I hoped there would be a last minute change of heart." He paused for breath a little lost for words. *"But what could I do, at the end of the day it was between the two of you and then Helen's final decision."*

At this point, although it was difficult to tell, it sounded to Neil as though Ron's voice was breaking up with emotion. Ron tried to continue and hiding his sadness said, *"So that's it she's gone, we have both lost her. Look I have to go. See you soon."*

He cut the conversation short, knowing his voice had started going squeaky and put the phone down almost before Neil had a chance to say goodbye. Could this business-like straight-to-the-point boss, firm but fair, man of the world, be in tears?

Neil did, of course, keep his doctor's appointment and as suspected was given the all clear to go back to work.

He often thought about Helen and how things might have been but it was now with an acceptance. He also often thought of Fiona and had learned, or thought he had, a lot earlier in his life the acceptance required to deal with his grief. He may or may not get over losing

Helen. He would never get over losing Fiona. He had however learned that he had to accept things. He just could not change the circumstance so he had to get on with his life. It was at this point he finally stopped smoking.

With his new acceptance, he was determined not to spend time thinking about his lost loves. He would instead fill his mind with other things. Read another book. Go out for another jog. Take up cycling again and bring back a little bit of his youth.

Neil did try very hard to be disciplined and keep his mind on the here and now. If ever he started to think about Fiona or Helen he made sure to dwell on the good times. That way he was able to think about them both, without starting to feel down. Realising what a very bumpy period the last couple of months or so had been he felt quite pleased with the way he had eventually dealt with it. He had regained his self-worth and his confidence and was actually looking forward to his future.

That night he kissed the photographs of Fiona and Helen. Thanked God for his goodness and lastly, before falling to sleep he said out loud...

"Tomorrow is the very first day of the rest of my life."

EPILOGUE: The Last Chapter.

Neil was feeling great. He had, in the past, always been an optimist. The light exercise and plenty of rest he had been getting lately had done him the world of good. All this and his faith had allowed him to get on top of his emotional problems and, all in all, he could see a good life ahead of him. What that life would consist of he did not know but he promised himself he would do everything to remain in control of it. He was back to work on Monday and looking forward to it in his old positive way.

'I think I ought to try and move on within the company' he decided. 'I will discuss this with Ron on Monday and with his advice, I will apply for an appropriate training course to improve my skills and knowledge. That way I may be in line for more promotion.'

He was going to try to stop letting the tides of life decide his direction and start taking matters into his own hands. He seemed to have been tossed about like seaweed in the waves, moving in any direction that life happened to take him. Now he was determined to move his life in the direction he wished to take. Make it good, in self-satisfaction, job satisfaction and self-worth. Become more financially sound. Do more, be more and have more, after all, he was worth it. Perhaps he could also give more. Be of greater use to his employer. Get more involved with the church and help out there. As far as relationships were concerned he knew that he could not manufacture love but he would certainly try to do a better job of hanging on to it if it came around again.

[27th March 1966]

Today was a beautiful day. No, the sun wasn't shining; it was just the way he felt. In fact, the temperature had plummeted and it had started to rain, with a bit of sleet mixed in. Yet, he was on top of the world. He recalled one of his favourite sayings 'It doesn't matter if it is raining outside as long as the sun is shining in your heart.' He thought about that for a moment and decided the saying was equally, if not more, appropriate if it became 'It doesn't matter if it is raining outside as long as the **Son** is shining in your heart.'

He just fancied a walk. 'Nothing too energetic today' he said to himself. Despite the rain, it was only a shower, the sky seemed bright, the birds were singing and the sun was doing its best to shine. What better than a nice slow walk along the beach to take in some of Gods wondrous creation?

He got wrapped up well, it was winter after all and the temperature had dropped in recent days. During the winter months, ever since childhood, he wore a vest only casting it once May was out, as Aunty Annie always said. So on top of that and his shirt he donned a polo-necked jumper, a jacket and a thick warm overcoat. The rain had eased now but it was very, very, cold out there; but off he went, with a spring in his step, for some more light exercise.

He seemed so up for it, more positive than for many a long day it was a new desire for life no matter what it would throw at him. His senses appeared to be almost on high alert although he was quite calm. Today he was able to perceive everything around him with a heightened sense of awareness. It was almost as if previously he had been deaf, dumb and blind or desensitised to the world.

You have probably experienced the sensation of not being totally aware of a noise until someone switches it off and suddenly there is a loud silence. It was like that today. He could see, hear, smell, touch and taste more, it seemed, than he had for such a long time. Many things, over the last year or so, seemed not to exist. Today he heard, saw and delighted in the experience of children playing, waves crashing, and seagulls screeching. There was the tempting smell of food emanating from restaurants. The stench of petrol and exhaust fumes from vehicles on the road nearby followed by the welcome relief of refreshing salt air filling his nostrils and lungs as he took to the beach.

He brushed his hands along the wall, yes, his favourite wall and could feel, as if for the first time, the rough surface of the stones and the sharp razor-like edges around the sides. Even his taste buds seemed to detect an extra mintiness from the Polo he sucked on. He was so alive and loving every minute.

He could not help though, just spending a little time, wondering about Helen. 'She is probably, about now, in Southampton boarding the ship or perhaps has already set sail for her new life in Australia. He had fully recovered emotionally but that did not mean there was no desire for her return. Even now he had perhaps a silly thought, more of a wish that 'She might change her mind? Perhaps she is walking towards me on the beach right now. She knows I like sitting here.' He looked towards the pier past the lifeboat station then to his right down the beach of the South Bay peering into the distance for a sight of her. 'What are the chances of that?' he mused 'I am really clutching at straws now.'

Yes he was clutching at straws I'm afraid. It is quite sad as at this point. It would have been a wonderfully happy and appropriate ending, considering the title of this story, to have them meet once more on the shore and at the end of the day walking off into the sunset arm in arm. But hey! It wasn't to be.

He remembered, as he sat there, the time he was taken by surprise in this very spot and wondered if even half expected, he would feel a hand on his shoulder and ***"Nice day!"*** being shouted out. He even looked behind him to check.

He returned his observation to the seashore noticing things that he would normally have paid little or no attention to. The debris on the beach, patterns in the sand left by the ebb tide and a child's bucket and spade that had been lost by some holiday making family who had somehow, long before the season had started, played on this part of the shoreline. They were sticking up out of the sand as if to shout 'Help! Here I am. Come back and find me, quick, before the tide comes in.'

He was aware of a ship and a couple of boats on the sea, looking like stand up cardboard pictures on the horizon from one of those children's books where the page expands outwardly using clever folds in the paper when the page is opened up.
'I wonder if that ship is going to Australia.' Then reprimanded himself 'Don't be silly Australian bound ships wouldn't be in this part of the North Sea. The Fairsea certainly wouldn't be in this area because Helen was boarding it in Southampton.'

Neil sat there for quite some time, enjoying the scene. The weather had brightened up a bit more although it was still very cold. 'Stranger on the Shore' he said to himself and chuckled, as he thought of that first meeting with Helen very near to here and the second one exactly at this spot. He remembered the many hours spent chatting over coffee in Luigi's. Especially their first visit to Spinetti's together. 'It is a wonder we did not suffer from caffeine poisoning' he mused 'that's if there is such a thing' He remembered when someone played their tune on the jukebox 'That was a very popular tune, by Aker Bilk if I remember rightly. It would be a good title for a book[16]' he reflected.

'I wonder if there are any lyrics[17] to the tune,' Neil contemplated.
Neil sat in his favourite spot for a long time, mulling things over in his mind. Thinking about his future and thinking positively about his next objective. He was getting a little too cold now to stay in one place and was just about to make his way home but on impulse decided instead to go into town.

He looked in just about every shop window and entered one or two of the stores, probably to get warmed up, but not for shopping. Whilst it would appear that he was not heading in any particular direction he found himself near to a very familiar place. He called in for a coffee at their, well now just **his**, favourite cafe. The thought of a warm frothy coffee was very inviting on this still very cold day. It may have been just to get warm but I have a sneaky feeling it was also for 'old time's sake.'

He began his long steep walk knowing that his reward would be a tasty warming mug of frothy coffee. Luigi greeted him in his usual friendly if not a little reluctant way. His past experience with this particular customer and his drinking partner had left him with mixed feelings. He keeps getting flashbacks of disturbances like fists banging on tables, cups spilt, dramatic scenes of unrequited love, heated discussions, crying fits etc. But they have been good customers and, well, providing they behaved themselves in future he was happy to keep taking their money.

"No Mrs-a with-a you today?" enquired Luigi rather hoping in some ways for the negative.

"No. You won't be seeing her again I am afraid. She has immigrated to Australia."
He did not bother to explain she wasn't his Mrs. *"She will be on the high seas this very moment."*

"Oh! I am-a so sorry to hear-a that" his attitude changing to sincere sorrow when he realised what that meant in lost revenue.

Neil started to feel very cold despite having several layers of clothing to protect him. No longer producing the same bodily warmth having stopped walking, he rubbed his hands together to try and create some heat. 'I am looking forward to this coffee, even if it is just in order to warm my hands,' he decided.

"It feels very cold in here Luigi. I had hoped to escape the cold weather when I got in here," Neil complained.

"Yes-a I am-a very-a sorry the heating it-a broke-a," answered Luigi with a look of apology on his face. *"The man-a said he couldn't-a come-a till tomorrow. I am-a very-a sorry."*

Luigi's genuine apology was accepted and Neil sat down in the busiest part of the cafe where there were lots of customers. He was aware that each human generates and gives off the same amount of heat as a single bar electric fire. So trying not to appear as being a bit of a weirdo he sat as near as he could to the tables that were surrounded by the greatest number of customers. Neil made sure his clothes were buttoned up properly and covered his body as best they could, started to drink his coffee, and was thankful for the warmth of the mug.

'Oh! That is really good' he said after his first sip. As he started to feel a little more comfortable and at least a little warmer he began to relax. As his focus was no longer entirely on trying to keep warm his eyes wandered around the room. Despite the cold, he still felt on top of the world and seemed to delight at watching the other customers. Some, like him, were concentrating on keeping warm and one customer was physically shaking, he assumed, with the freezing temperature. Then there were the parents trying to keep their children in check. Some of the children did not appear to be affected by the cold at all.

Halfway through his coffee, his attention was caught by a notice on the wall from a training college and he began to write down the telephone number. Constantine Technical College in Middlesbrough was offering HNC courses in Metallurgy. 'It may not be exactly what I am looking for but you never know. It is worth writing the contact number down and talking it over with Ron,' he decided to make a note of it. Due to the layers of clothing, this was a little more of a complicated manoeuvre than usual. Eventually, he took out a pen from his shirt pocket, paper from his wallet, and then quickly buttoned himself up again. It was so cold he could see his steaming breath like a cloud hovering in the air.

'Middlesbrough is a fair drag from here but it would be worth the effort,' he decided. Then he realised a problem. The cost of fees and travel expenses could be too much for me to afford. He mulled this over for some time 'Unless Ron knows of another training organisation based closer to Scarborough' but finally settled for drastic action to achieve his goal. 'I can always sell my Ford Cortina and buy a motorbike. Perhaps a Norton or a Royal Enfield' he mused. In fact, he actually thought it might be fun having a motorbike. 'It would be cheaper all round' he decided. The thought also crossed his mind that Ron may be willing to foot the bill.

He put the piece of paper with the phone number, along with his pen, into the top pocket of his jacket and again quickly wrapped himself up. He was certainly a lot warmer now. The cafe had filled right up with lots of other people coming in, out of the freezing cold, only to be shocked at finding there was no heating system in operation. Still, some of the best 'central heating' or **central eating** is food and drink. He kept his hands around his mug draining it of the last remnants of heat as he sat thinking what he should have this evening to eat. 'I think there is some football on the telly. I might just have a takeaway and a couple of bottles of beer tonight.'
He sat for a while feeling a little reluctant to get up and go. 'It may be cold in here' he thought, 'but it will be a lot colder out there.' Still warming his hands on the now tepid mug he encouraged himself to make a move. 'Come on, finish your coffee and let's brave the weather.'

He took the last mouthful of coffee.....but immediately spat it straight out halfway across the room with a sudden surprise. The coffee wasn't cold, it wasn't bitter; he spat it out because of the huge shock that had just greeted him. He had just seen something that he never ever believed he would see. So shocked was he that he stood up like a rocket. His chair shot back into a passing waitress sending her and her tray of food sprawling over a table and its customers who all got served, a bit quicker than they expected, but not as proficiently as they had expected.

Neil's table was flung over and cup, saucer, spoon, sugar bowl and anything else in the vicinity found itself flying through the air. This was complete uproar and chaos. Customers were shouting, some groaning, as they tried to wipe the food off their face and clothing.

He ignored the devastation that was all around him ran towards the exit and at the same time spread his arms to the widest extent possible and shouted......

"Helen!" as he rushed to embrace her.

Helen had just opened the door and was standing looking around on the off chance that Neil would be there. He was and had certainly made himself obvious to her as he bounded across the cafe knocking over more of the furniture and causing other customers to cower for fear of getting the same treatment they had just seen those nearest to him receive.

He was naturally very pleased to see her and his enthusiasm overflowed. Once again chaos reigned in Spinetti's. People moved out of the way while others just sat there dripping with food. Some people got up and left, well, tried to because the door was blocked by our two heroes clasped together in the biggest and longest of hugs.

"You're-a barred, you're-a barred, get outa of-a my-a cafe, you're-a barred." Luigi had had enough. He was hopping mad and ran across the room to physically push them out of the door, ***"And-a don't-a come-a back."*** Again he repeated, as he shut the door behind them. ***"And-a don't-a come-a back."*** Looking at them with daggers through the door window. The door was again opened, this time by irate customers filing out and some of them shouting abuse which was particularly directed at Neil.

Luigi was still chuntering to himself as he helped the staff to clean up the mess. Still looking at and talking towards the door, as if they were still in sight. He began again, *"Anda don't-a come-a backa, you are not-a welcome, you're-a barred, you're-a barred, I willa not-a have-a this in-a my-a cafe, chunter-a, chunter-a, chunter-a."*

To say that customers were not very pleased is a huge understatement. Luigi carried on trying to clear up the mess and once he had stopped his tirade of threats aimed at Neil and Helen who were too far away to hear him anyway, he turned to his customers to apologise and kept repeating, *"I am-a so sorry, I am-a so sorry."*

Even before they had finished their embrace which continued during and after their eviction from Spinetti's, Neil had asked what seemed like a hundred questions without giving Helen a chance to answer one of them.

"Are you OK?" "What's happened?" "Are you back for good?"

Still clasped together they started to walk, not consciously choosing a direction just quickly moving away from Luigi's wrath and irate noisy customers who, the last time they looked, were still piling out of the cafe and giving very disgusted looks and making threatening and sometimes very vulgar gestures towards the happy couple.

Hurrying along the street even faster, sensing the annoyance from behind, Neil continued...

"Have you changed your mind?" "Does your dad know your back?" "Do you love me?"

Even after that question, the most important one of them all, Helen was not given time to answer.

"Yes," she replied firmly. But more questions rained down on her.

"Yes!" said Helen again, but louder this time, trying to interrupt an ever-increasing avalanche of questions. Eventually clasping her hand around his mouth, and standing still refusing to move, despite the threat from behind, she got through to him.

"Yes, I do love you."

That, at last, shut him up and once he realised what she had said he started to listen intently. The last of the hostile customers had now lost interest in pursuing them. Also, there was a break in the torrent of Neil's enthusiastic questioning so Helen started to explain. *"I changed my mind. When I got to my friends in London I thought long and hard about what I was doing. I just couldn't leave you. After all, we had gone through, separately and together, the truth was that we both still loved each other. Even though I had put a lot of effort, both physically and emotionally, into going to Australia and the reality of a new life was within my grasp, I just couldn't do it."*

Another warm embrace ensued and a kiss that was both longed for and full of promise. They were still in the middle of the street. Not on the road but in full public view on the pavement. Neil broke away and tried to take off his overcoat. His hands were numb with the cold and he was so excited that his fingers didn't seem to want to function properly and eventually he gave up trying to unbutton it and almost ripped it off. The coat was putting up a good fight and did not want to go quietly.

While struggling with his overcoat he now also struggled with his words *"Look..., let me..., you must see this..., wait just a minute."* His overcoat now seemed to have him in some sort of wrestling hold rather like an arm lock.

The two of them were blocking the path of shoppers in the middle of town. Neil still fighting with his clothing as one or two people stopped to watch what was going on. Gone were any sign of Luigi's customers but another group, this time of unsuspecting shoppers had started to gather.

Having finally managed to divest himself of his wrestling overcoat, by giving it a body slam on the pavement, he now struggled with his jacket.

*"What **are** you doing?"* questioned Helen in a rather worried voice.

He was so excited and so hyped up that the act of undressing was just not as easy as normal. Of course, his hands were now very cold indeed which made it even more difficult as his fingers were on strike, or at least a go slow.

The crowd grew larger as he tore at his jacket. It finally surrendered and was swung around his head and flung up into the air where it wrapped itself around a lamppost. Now for his polo neck jumper, *"Help me with this Helen,"* Neil pleaded as he had got it over his head but the neck got stuck on his ears and refused to move any further.

Despite her verbal objections she seemed obliged to help. Reluctantly she grabbed his jumper and pulled hard. So hard she almost pulled him over but it did the trick and she dropped it to the ground on his overcoat.

'What on earth is he going to do now?' thought Helen hoping he wasn't planning on stripping off in the street. She was ready to intervene if he went for his trouser belt.

"I have something to show you.... err give you," blustered Neil trying to undo his shirt collar buttons.

'The mind boggles.' Yes Helen's mind was boggling. She knew he could be impulsive and did not really know what to expect next. With a crowd gathering, some pedestrians had now got to walk on the road to get around them, causing cars and cyclists to swerve. **"Don't take your clothes off, not here!"** she said.

"Oh yes!" announced Neil, *"I have been waiting for this for a long time and I can't wait any longer."*

Just as Helen thought she had better put a stop this. She had visions of them both being arrested. Neil, violently unbuttoned his shirt causing some of the buttons to pop off and shoot into the air. He then put his hand down the inside of his vest and pulled out a chain which fell in front of his shirt. It was a long chain which he removed from around his neck. There, on the chain, was her diamond engagement ring. He had worn it since the day she rejected it and him, in the cafe.

By now an even bigger crowd had gathered and although starting to feel a little embarrassed Helen was so engrossed in what Neil was doing she was determined to stay put regardless.

Neil fell on both knees. It's normally just one knee but as that did not work last time he thought two might swing it. He then asked with tears of joy in his eyes.

"Please, please will you marry me now?"

Whilst Helen's instinct was to answer immediately with an emphatic 'YES' she thought the moment deserved a little heightened drama just like they do when the results of a competition are read out. **[Those reality shows with the telephone votes that are now shown on our modern television programmes use the same idea although they always seem to overdo it.]**

So she paused for dramatic effect looking around at the crowd. Some of them were smiling and nodding their heads as if willing her to say yes. It wasn't a long pause. Seeing the look of hope and expectation in Neil's eyes melted her heart and brought forth the answer he was seeking.

"Yes! Yes, I will marry you."

The whole crowd began to cheer. Pedestrians spilt off the pavement into the street as cars skidded to a stop trying to avert an accident. Neil put the ring on her finger to loud applause, cheers, shouts, whoops and pats on the back from their audience. Neil and Helen hugged and kissed then began shaking hands with everyone around them. Whilst this was far from normal it just seemed so right that everyone in the world had joined in the celebration.

The crowds slowly dispersed having enjoyed the spectacle. Neil had not felt the cold while performing his striptease but now began to shiver as he got dressed, retrieving his clothing from the pavement and nearby lamppost. It was just as well because the police had been informed of the disturbance, causing traffic problems, and were now approaching the scene.

Neil was now properly dressed and Helen was still admiring the ring long after the crowd had gone. The traffic had got back to normal and the couple could see the police approaching.

The officers gave a rather knowing look towards the newly engaged couple as they passed. They had been watching the event from a distance and as they got closer thought, 'we will probably have to arrest these two if they are not willing to stop doing whatever was causing the disruption.' The constables received an equally knowing look in return from Neil and Helen as if to say 'yes it was us officer, but somehow we just don't care.'

As there was now no problem, no disturbance to break up the officers took no action and just continued to walk down the street away from the culprits. So too did Neil and Helen, in the opposite direction to the police. They uttered a sigh of relief *"Phew"* after the police had passed them, and kept walking, realising they had probably escaped arrest or at least a telling off by the skin of their teeth.

A few yards down the road they did have a cheeky look back to see what the officers were doing and carried on walking and laughing out loud as they realised what a close call it was, what fun it was, but most of all how happy they were.

They walked and walked and walked, and talked and talked and talked, stopping often to kiss. *"Let's go on the beach,"* Helen suggested in a happy moment of silliness on such a cold day. Soon they found themselves sitting on Neil's favourite seaside wall. During their walk, all of Neil's questions had been answered. All his prayers, well at least those he knew were possible, had also been answered.

"It is very beautiful," said Helen, admiring her engagement ring again.

"Well, I am glad you like it. It cost me six attempts on the hoopla stall, in the arcade to win that," joked Neil.....

.....*and*, they all lived happily ever after. [Well you know it never actually works out quite like that, only in fairy tales.] However, the problems of the future were nothing compared to those they had left behind. They got married, found true love and happiness together, and gave Ron, Neil's new father-in-law, those grandchildren he wanted. This was to everyone's delight but also Helen's relief remembering her previous bleak childbearing days.

They both moved into and purchased the house that Helen had been renting which fortunately was still on the market.

Helen began attending church with Neil. It may have been just to please Neil at least to start with. But hey! That doesn't matter, she decided. 'In order to learn about it, I need to get involved.' She realised that 'One can only make an *informed* judgement if one is *informed*.'

Helen began to get more interested and gradually understood what it was all about. One of the friends she made at church made a remark that finally convinced her to become a Christian. It was pointed out to Helen that if she read the New Testament and replaced the word 'Jesus' with the word 'love,' and vice versa, it would have the same meaning. The two words, in the context of the New Testament, were interchangeable.

She also realised that it was not necessary to understand everything. She had learned that no explanation is needed for a believer and that no amount of explanation is enough for those who do not wish to believe. She took that step of faith.

There was just one thing that stuck in her throat. As she was a divorcee she was quite sad that the vicar could not allow them a church wedding[18]. They were given a church blessing and that was beautiful.

It turned out that Neil did not need to sell his prized Ford Cortina after all. He was generally better off financially because Helen was, as you know, already quite well fixed. Ron was very enthusiastic about Neil improving his skills and so paid the course fees and allowed him one day a week off work to attend the Constantine Technical College in Middlesbrough. He was successful in gaining an HNC followed by an LIM course. Within five years of his successful courses, he was made a director of Crosby's Aluminium Foundry. This may have had something to do with him being Ron's son-in-law. But Ron, being a businessman, would not have offered a directorship to anyone who did not cut the mustard. Neil had passed with flying colours and went on to do great things for the company. This of course benefitted, Ron, Helen, himself, his family, along with all the other workers within the foundry.

Luigi Spinetti forgave them for the chaos in his cafe and let them back in after they sent him a letter of apology and an explanation. This was accompanied by a bottle of good wine and an invitation to their wedding. They paid for his breakages and treated him to a slap up meal at the best restaurant in town. They became very good friends with Luigi after that. Mind you he still gets a little panicky whenever they call in for their usual frothy coffees.

THE END

REFERENCES

1. Life Boat Station was comparatively recently knocked down and replaced on the same site.
2. D.A. stands for Ducks Arse.
3. C of E used by many as a cop out. Coming to church only for special occasions. My faith tells me God still loves them and is delighted when anyone comes to church, for whatever reason.
4. 'Music While you Work'; This particular programme was well known for quick, up-tempo, music so that workers across the country were encouraged to work faster. Yes, I am not kidding, that was some of the reasoning, by the programme-makers, behind the choice of music.
5. Yes there was such a thing in those days both £1 and 10 shilling paper money. Ten shillings was comparatively speaking a lot of money. In today's money it is only 50p.
6. Today I think the meaning of the word **Camp** is different to Neil's days. So no, Camp Coffee was not intended for people, who were of a different sexual persuasion to the norm.
7. Later to be known as **the Great Train Robbery.** Not because there was anything good about it but because of the huge amount of money stolen. Also possibly the size of the operation. Men, vehicles and planning.
8. L.P. stands for Long Playing record. A large vinyl disc played at 33 and one third revolutions per minute.
9. **Seat-Belts**. It wasn't until 1983 that the wearing of front seatbelts became law. In 1989 the law insisted that children under 14 had to wear a rear seat belt. The government waited until 1991 to make the same rule for adults sitting in the back. Of course, since then stricter rules have come into force so that small children are strapped into safety seats.
10. The nearside is the passenger side of the car.
11. Paramnesia: A disorder of the memory or
the faculty of recognition in which dreams may be confused with reality. A condition or phenomenon involving distorted

memory or confusions of fact and fantasy, such as confabulation. Confabulation is a symptom of various memory disorders in which made-up stories fill in any gaps in memory.

12. The Lounge, is sometimes called the 'front room' up north.
13. I remember as a very young boy using the toilets on Darlington High Row. Seeing that notice, 'Please adjust your dress.' I thought, 'what a silly sign, boys don't wear dresses.'
14. Doctors in those days operated by allowing patients to come in without an appointment and sit in the waiting room and wait in turn to see the doctor. Neil's doctor it seems was ahead of its time and required patients to make an appointment.
15. Barbiturates; In those day's doctors were not yet aware that Barbiturates actually made some people feel suicidal and tipped many people who were on the edge right over it.
16. Book; Yes, two great minds think alike. In fact, I believe there has been more than one book with that title though very different stories.
17. Lyrics; Yes there are lyrics to 'Stranger on the Shore' but they are not telling Neil's story. They are nothing like Neil's story apart from the odd very rare coincidental similarity.
18. This applied to all Church of England Vicars at that time. This ruling has only comparatively recently been relaxed.

THE AUTHOR: Leon Franklin

When I started to write this, my first story, Stranger on the Shore, in 2013, I was well into my sixties. I was born in the North East of England. I have lived in the same area all my life. Well, not quite all my life because the last time I checked I was still in the land of the living.

I was born in the late '40s and lived as a young person, including some of my teenage years, through the '60s and feel very fortunate to have done so. It was a wonderful era. Not just for me but I think for the British in general. Of course, everyone has a different perception of the same events and I am sure there will be some people that had a terrible time.

From my memory, as a teenager, the Teddy-Boy rage was, just to say, still apparent. They wore long Edwardian style jackets, drainpipe trousers, lace ties, very thick soled suede shoes and each had a DA hairstyle. Into the ascendant came the mods and rockers. Rockers wore lots of leather and rode motorbikes. I was a mod. Mods generally rode Vespa Scooters but I never did. I think I must have been a bit of a rocker because I wanted a motorbike but my Dad said no. Although I was not too happy at the time, looking back, I am really pleased he said no. Very dangerous!

As a mod, I liked the very smart clothes. I just know I looked really good in my Italian style suit, Slim-Jim tie and winkle picker shoes. Noel Edmonds still wears shoes like that. You know the ones with the pointed toes and raised heels.

I remember once being stopped by a policeman. He said, *"Tell me, sonny, do your toes go all the way to the end of those shoes?"* I said, *"No officer. Does your head go all the way to the top of your helmet?"*
In those days the police wore tall pointy hats, not the flat caps they usually wear now. Actually, that was just a joke. In those days most youngsters had respect for people in authority, including parents. Most of us would never speak to people like that, even if we thought it, even as a joke.

In my childhood, I found a wonderful love, rather like the relationship between Fiona and Neil in my story. Not the same story and not the same events but the relationship and love between Neil and Fiona was almost identical to ours. June and I were childhood sweethearts, and I lost her to cancer. She was 12 and I was 14 when we met. I was forty she was thirty-eight when she died. One day I may write my story.

I must be mad, writing any story when I am really not qualified to do so. I have never until just recently, taken any formal training as a writer and the only English test I ever took was at school and I failed it. Having read the book you may already have guessed that. ☺

You see, to start with - I nevar waz goode at spellin...
So far I have had no professional help. I have relied on my computer spellchecker, and of course, friends, relations and other volunteers doing checks. If it wasn't for them I would not even contemplate sending this to a proof-reader or a publisher unless I knew someone that wanted a good laugh.

If you have this book in your hands properly printed and bound, whether from a library, a bookshop, as a present, from a jumble sale or retrieved from someone's skip, you can at least be sure that I did find a publisher who liked it.

It is now 2019 and although at first I had no plans to self-publish, I have changed my mind and I have decided to donate any profits from the sale of this book to Friends of St. Clare's. By visiting my website leonfranklin.org or friendsofstclares.uk you can find out more about it. Friends of St. Clare's is a charitable organisation set up to support the church.

If indeed this book does start to sell I do hope you send me your comments. Tell me as much about the experience as you can, as well as obvious things, like how much you enjoyed it or otherwise. I would like to have feedback on things such as writing style. Were you happy when I spoke directly to you the reader? Were the paragraphs too long or perhaps too short? Did I use too many long words that ordinary people will not understand? More than likely, in my case, the words were probably not long, unusual, or sophisticated enough.

That last sentence has just stopped me in my tracks. After typing the word sophisticated, I was shocked to see that my spelling was correct! I am now wondering if my spellchecker is working properly. I hope I haven't worn it out. Anyway back to the plot.

Was the storyline fast moving? Was it ever boring? I think you know the sort of criticism I mean. I will only learn through criticism so bring it on. You can contact me via my website: leonfranklin.org

If you enjoyed **Stranger on the Shore...** Please tell all your friends and relations.

If not.
Please tell me...

Leonfranklin.org

ACKNOWLEDGEMENTS AND EXTRAS

Although my story is fictional I did wherever possible endeavour to make the events dates and places as factual as possible. I wish to thank and acknowledge the following organisations and/or persons for their help with my research.

GARDEN MUSEUM
Guidance on the price of flowers in the '60s
Russell Clark, Curator of Exhibitions. Garden Museum. London. SE1 7LB
Mobile 07852929093 : Telephone 020 7401 8865
http://www.gardenmuseum.org.uk/

ENCYCLOPAEDIA BRITTANICA (UK) LTD
Registered in England and Wales: Number 3830890
Re: Great Train Robbery Information
http://www.britannica.com/EBchecked/topic/243830/Great-Train-Robbery

LISTEN TO THE MUSIC
Acker Bilks, Stranger on the Shore
https://www.youtube.com/watch?v=7jzx664u5DA&list=RD7jzx664u5DA&start_radio=1
The Beatles Second Album
https://www.youtube.com/watch?v=Hz5jXwOXgKQ&list=PL7KzgqJq2IfKyv377F0MvQp3-mhy1CM-f&index=2
Calling All Workers
http://www.youtube.com/watch?v=RMEpjDFHN50

THE ASHES
http://en.wikipedia.org/wiki/The_Ashes

TEN POUND POMS
https://collections.museumsvictoria.com.au/search?query=Liner+Fairsea

ROYAL SOCIETY FOR THE PREVENTION OF ACCIDENTS
RoSPA House, Edgbaston Park, 353 Bristol Road, Birmingham B5 7ST.
Telephone: 0121 248 2000 Fax: 0121 248 2001
Email: help@rospa.com
https://www.rospa.com/
Registered Charity No: 207823

YORK
Photographs of Browns Department Store York.
To view these and lots of others visit my website www.leonfranklin.org
Thank you to Paul Stabler and Angela Horner Directors Browns Department Stores. Davygate, York, YO1 8QT
http://www.brownsyork.co.uk/

SNICKELWAYS OF YORK
http://www.yorkshireguides.com/snickelways.html

NATIONAL AIR AND SPACE MUSEUM
The world's first space rendezvous.
https://airandspace.si.edu/stories/editorial/worlds-first-space-rendezvous

SUSAN STANWIX
For useful information and local knowledge about Northallerton. Click the link and scroll down looking for South Parade to read her memories.
http://www.francisfrith.com/northallerton/memories/

> NOTE: The links in this book to websites have been checked. However please accept my apologies if you find difficulty with any of them.

Acknowledgements and extras continued next page…

ALUMINIUM

Extensive information on the Aluminium Industry in the 60's and appropriate training courses.

Dr David A. Harris of the Aluminium Advocates Consultancy, based in Oxfordshire.

Dr David A. Harris, CEng, FIMMM.
www.alfed.org.uk

Constantine Technical College
The College majored on metallurgy and engineering in the early years. It became Teesside Polytechnic in 1969 and then became Teesside University in 1992. They offered a part-time HNC course in metallurgy and almost certainly also offered an LIM course for those successful at HNC who wished to study further.

Dr David Harris pictured with a replica of the historic "Diane de Gabies" statue, presented to him by ALFED in November 2008 as a Lifetime Achievement Award.

As a student, David Harris was sponsored through University by a major aluminium company.

He graduated with an Honours degree and PhD. He spent three years as a University lecturer, teaching Materials Science to engineering undergraduates, before joining Alcan Australia as Technical Manager for Rolled and Ingot Products Division. Returning to the UK, he ran the Association of Light Alloy Refiners organisation and then, for some twenty years, was CEO of Aluminium Federation.